HOUSE OF THE RED FISH

ALSO AVAILABLE FROM LAUREL-LEAF BOOKS

GRAHAM SALISBURY

Aloha!

Graham Salib

HOUSE OF THE
RED FISH

LAUREL-LEAF BOOKS

Published by Laurel-Leaf
an imprint of Random House Children's Books
a division of Random House, Inc.
New York

This is a work of fiction. Names, characters, places, and incidents
either are the product of the author's imagination or are used
fictitiously. Any resemblance to actual persons, living or dead,
events, or locales is entirely coincidental.

Originally published in hardcover in the United States by
Wendy Lamb Books, New York, in 2006. This edition published
by arrangement with Wendy Lamb Books.

Laurel-Leaf and colophon are registered trademarks
of Random House, Inc.

www.randomhouse.com/teens

Educators and librarians, for a variety of teaching tools,
visit us at www.randomhouse.com/teachers

RL: 5.2
ISBN: 978-0-440-23838-6
January 2008
Printed in the United States of America
10 9 8 7 6 5 4 3 2 1
First Laurel-Leaf Edition

FOR
YOUNG PEOPLE EVERYWHERE

FOLLOW YOUR DREAMS
NEVER GIVE UP

✢ ✢ ✢

<u>MAHALO NUI LOA</u>
ROBYN SALISBURY,
TAKAKO KYO,
AND
GLENNA RHODES

HOUSE OF THE
RED FISH

1
IN THE BEFORE TIME

One Saturday morning in September 1941, three months before the Japanese bombed Pearl Harbor, the islands lay on the ocean as warm and peaceful as cats sleeping in the sun. Life was still good then, and I'd just started eighth grade at Roosevelt High School.

I woke with a jolt, threw on a pair of shorts and a shirt, and ran out of the house, letting the screen door slap behind me. "You need to eat something!" Mama called, coming up to peer through the screen.

"Later," I said, turning to jog backwards.

She waved me off and sank back into the darkness of the house.

Papa was coming in today. He and his deckhand, Sanji, had been gone for a week, fishing for tuna somewhere beyond the blue horizon.

I jumped on a city bus and headed down to Kewalo Basin, the harbor where Papa kept his boat. When I got there the *Taiyo Maru* sat motionless alongside the pier, its fish unloaded and Papa and Sanji hosing down a week's worth of fish slime. She was a beautiful boat, bright white to match her name—the *Sun*—a Japanese-style fishing sampan thirty-eight feet long.

"Heyyy," Sanji said as I jogged up. "Look who's here, boss. Better put um to work, ah? Make um more fast for me to get home to see my girls." He meant Reiko, his wife, and their three-year-old daughter, Mari, the two people he lived for. Sanji was only nineteen, by far the youngest father I knew.

"Tomi," Papa said, a big grin on his face. "We cleaning up. Come aboard."

That was exactly what I wanted to do. To work with Papa and Sanji on the *Taiyo Maru* was one of my dreams. That and playing baseball. In all of life, what else was there besides boats and baseball?

Papa stood with his feet spread, coiling a rope. Dark brown from a lifetime on the sea, short haircut, baggy khaki pants. And that grin.

"You catch much?" I asked.

He wagged his eyebrows. "Best haul we ever had."

"Ho, really?"

"Got lucky, this time. The guy counting us our money right now."

Sanji tossed me a scrub brush.

An hour later, the boat was squeaky clean. All the equipment was stored in the hold, and the deck was free of fish slime and smelling good again. Sanji jumped off onto the pier and untied the lines. He tossed them over to me. "You know what to do with this ropes?"

"Pfff," I said. "As good as you, any day."

He laughed. "You dreaming, cockaroach."

He looked up at Papa, still on the boat. "Hey, boss, try go get the small glass ball. I forgot um in the drawer by the deckhouse."

Papa dug it out and held it up.

"That's for you," Sanji said to me. "I foun' um about ten miles pas' Kauai. Keep um. I give you."

Papa handed me the glass ball.

"Ho, thanks, Sanji." I held the green net float from Japan up to the sun. Every time I touched one I thought of that far-away country my family came from—Japan, trapped inside the glass, its mystery magnified by the sun. Every now and then you could find them in the ocean, or washed up on the beach. If this one had been covered with barnacles like usual, Sanji had cleaned them off. "Like a good-luck charm," he said.

While Sanji went over to warm up his fish-stinky truck for the ride home, Papa and I walked the boat out into the harbor and tied it to its mooring, a white float chained to a giant block of concrete on the sand below.

Papa untied the small skiff he kept secured upside down on the bow. It made a plopping sound when he dropped it down onto the water. I eased over the side into it and set the glass ball on the floorboards. Papa handed me the wooden pigeon crate. He'd taken six of his pigeons to sea. "They all come home?" he asked.

"Right on time."

Papa smiled and lowered himself into the skiff, rocking it gently. Every time he went to sea he'd take some of his racing pigeons a few miles out and turn them loose to find their way home. They always did. And fast. Their homing instinct fascinated Papa and me. How they knew just where to go was a mystery, like how some animals get antsy minutes before an earthquake.

I sat in the stern facing Papa as he rowed long, slow strokes back to the pier. He dipped his head. "Look at that boat."

I turned back to gaze at the *Taiyo Maru*. She had an open deck with a small forward wheelhouse sitting on it like a queen. And a long-armed tiller that Papa often guided with his knee.

"It's a good one," I said.

"From way back in my younger days that's what I dreamed about . . . right there."

I studied it closer, this time noticing how it sat on the water, perfectly still and perfectly balanced, not tilting to one side like some boats in that harbor.

"It's a good boat," I said, unable to think of anything smarter to say.

Papa smiled and nodded.

Rowed.

Back at the pier Sanji helped us haul the skiff out and carry it over to the palm trees where the fishermen kept their skiffs. We turned it upside down and tucked the oars under it.

A man from the fish shed came out and handed Papa a wad of bills the size of a big fat riceball. "Good catch,

Nakaji," the guy said. "Do that again and you'll be a rich man."

"Already am," Papa said, putting his hand on my shoulder.

The guy winked at me and left.

Papa counted the money, his lips moving soundlessly. Sanji turned away to give him privacy.

"Unn," Papa grunted, handing Sanji his pay.

Sanji gaped. "This too much, boss." He tried to give some of it back.

Papa waved him off. "You worked hard. Buy gas for that rattrap truck. Take home something nice for Reiko and Mari."

Sanji ducked his head. "You too good to me, boss."

The three of us squeezed into the small cab of the truck for the ride home, the shiny green glass ball in my hands winking in the sunlight. It was the perfect day—except for the fish stink.

A small price for all we had.

In the before time.

2
THE
TAIYO MARU

Now it was Wednesday, March 3, 1943, a year and a half later.

My best friend Billy Davis and I had just finished another slow day of school, both of us now in ninth grade. Instead of heading home, I'd talked Billy into coming down to the Ala Wai Canal with me to stare at Papa's boat.

We hopped on a city bus to Kapiolani and Kamoku Street, then headed through a quiet neighborhood to the bushes and trees that hid the canal from view. From the trees we crossed a wide field of dirt, the afternoon sky blue and silky. Puffy white clouds sat like hats on the green mountaintops behind us.

We eased down at the edge of the Ala Wai, a rainwater drainage canal that wandered from the swampy lowlands out to the ocean, mixing rusty mud-water with the clean blue sea just past a small-boat harbor. To the right of that harbor, a manmade channel cut into the reef that edged the shore and ran parallel to the beach over to Kewalo Basin, where the *Taiyo Maru* had harbored before the war.

A silvery mullet jumped after some bug, then plopped back down, leaving rings that wobbled toward us, then vanished. Behind us, the muted sounds of Honolulu whispered through thick weeds sagging in the heat of the sun.

Billy tossed a pebble into the water. "This probably wasn't a great idea."

"Yeah, prob'ly."

Going down to the canal only brought back terrible memories of terrible days of just over a year ago. On December 7, 1941, the Japanese slammed down on Hawaii, bombed Pearl Harbor, and plunged us into war. Papa and Sanji were out fishing the day they came.

The next day two U.S. P-40 Tomahawks dropped out of the sky and came down on Papa's sampan with their machine guns blazing, wounding Papa in the leg and killing Sanji.

Of all that had happened, that was the worst.

Papa wounded and Sanji dead. Only nineteen, with a wife and little girl. I didn't even know who to blame—Japan or the U.S. Navy.

And then the navy raced a boat out and arrested Papa, threw him into a makeshift prison on Sand Island with blood still leaking into the T-shirt he'd wrapped around his torn-up leg.

The same day the U.S. Army confiscated his boat and towed it up into the Ala Wai Canal to rot.

A few days later, the FBI came up to our house and made

me kill Papa's pigeons. His beautiful, gentle birds. Then they arrested my Grampa Joji and took him away to who knew where. Just because he was a Japanese citizen.

Those days.

Out fishing, Papa and Sanji hadn't even known that Pearl Harbor had been attacked, or that they were supposed to have been flying an American flag to identify the boat as friendly when they came in. They had no radio. Who could afford one?

And what did the pigeons do that was so terrible the FBI had to kill them?

And what had Grampa Joji done, an old man who raised chickens?

That was all my family had. Fishing and chickens. It was how we lived.

Now, me and Mama and my five-year-old sister, Kimi, survived off the pennies Mama made as a housekeeper for the Wilsons, the rich family whose land we lived on. We stretched that money as far as it would go.

"You the man of the house now," Mama told me the day they took Grampa away. That night she'd cried, silent and alone in the war-darkened kitchen.

So many times after that day I'd said, "I can quit school and get a job." But she was firm. "No, Tomi-kun. You go school. Work summertime. We fine. School more important."

She wouldn't budge. "Work summertime."

Last summer I made a few dollars washing cars at the service station over by the grocery store. Maybe this year I'd work down at the pineapple cannery.

***

Me and Billy squatted on our heels at the edge of the canal, silent, barefoot, in long pants and loose shirts. What we wore to school. I was thinking I should have gone straight home, because this was Kimi's day, *Hinamatsuri,* or Dolls' Festival, the day my family celebrated a girl's growth and happiness.

But here I was at the canal again, staring at Papa's boat.

Underwater.

Sunk the day it was towed to this spot, we'd heard—a hole axed in the hull.

Even though it made me feel helpless, I kept coming back, because with Papa and Grampa Joji away in U.S. Army prison camps, looking down on the *Taiyo Maru* was my way of still being with them, the three of us together—grandfather, father, son. That sunken boat and two postcards we'd gotten from Papa was all I had of them.

I was thankful that Billy had come with me. He was the best friend I'd ever had. I was glad he'd convinced his parents he should stay at Roosevelt High for one more year, instead of changing schools and going to private school at Punahou like his brother, Jake. Billy liked Roosevelt. All his friends were there.

He stood a head taller than me now, blond, almost five-eleven. He could lift me up and set me on the hood of a jeep, if he wanted to. But I was strong, too, because every day I worked at lifting a thirty-pound boulder I found in a stream to build myself up for baseball. Also, I'd worked pulling up fish on Papa's boat. "Haw! Bonecrusher, you," Billy once said when I gripped his hand. "You could crush a tin can with that grip." Made me feel pretty good.

Across the water a blanket of trees smothered the jumble of low houses behind Waikiki. Just below us the canal sat rusty brown, with mullet nosing through the muck for food, waggling in and out of sight around Papa's boat.

"Looks kind of sad, doesn't it?" Billy said.

Moss fuzzed green on a coil of rope on the wood-planked deck.

I nodded.

The boat sat on the muddy bottom in about eight feet of water. Only a foot or two of its deckhouse stood above the surface. Its name, *Taiyo Maru,* was soberly lettered in black across its white stern transom, and bullet tracks trailed across the decking, a reminder of that dark day. That was the worst to look at—the bullet tracks. Sanji died right there on that deck, I thought. Papa must have crawled around with his bleeding leg trying to help him, to bring him back, looking up to see how far away the island was, searching for help . . . when Sanji was already gone.

"Tomi," Billy said. "You okay?"

I nodded, turning my face away.

Billy tossed another pebble into the water.

I was grateful for his silence.

The *Taiyo Maru* wasn't the only sunken boat here. There were ten of them, all Japanese fishing sampans.

I pinched the bridge of my nose.

"We got to stop coming here, Tomi," Billy said. "There's

nothing you can do. What's done is done. Brooding over it won't bring it back up."

Billy scooped up a handful of dirt and added, "Actually, the boat looks okay, you know . . . I mean, it's not all broken up or anything. It looks good."

"Except that it's on the bottom."

"Well, yeah, there's that."

All these boats had been in the canal for over a year. Before he was arrested Grampa told me the army chopped holes in them and sank them so they couldn't be used against us in the war. But I keep thinking . . . fishing boats? Small sampans? What harm could they do?

I peered into the water. How bad was the hole?

Maybe someday I'd dive down and take a look.

The other sampans wobbled under the surface nearby, the tops of their small deckhouses sitting on the water like gravestones, some straight up, some angled, sinking sideways.

I turned to look back over my shoulder, the world feeling eerily still, as if someone were sneaking up on us. But the wide field of dirt and weeds and the thick bushes that blocked the narrow streets and low buildings of Honolulu from view were as vacant as when we got there.

Billy skimmed a pebble across the water, where circles ballooned out and jiggled the clouds sleeping on the glassy surface. "Let's go home." He pushed himself up. "It's getting dark. Curfew's soon."

"Yeah," I said, but didn't move.

Billy crossed his arms and checked the sun, now easing toward the sea.

I picked up a stone and slammed it into the canal. If a wall had been there I would have hit it with my fist. "I can't help it, Billy. It's Papa's boat. It was all he had. How can I just leave it here to rot?"

"What can you do?"

A thought came flickering back, one that had popped up the day before while I was daydreaming in class. An impossible thought.

Wasn't it?

"I could bring it up."

Billy snorted. "And I can lift a car with my bare hands. Come on, we gotta get home."

I shrugged and stood. Yeah, what could I do, even if Billy helped me? Two ninth-grade kids.

"Let's *go*," Billy pleaded. "We gotta get home before curfew. You might not mind getting shot at, but I sure do."

We started across the dirt field, because Billy had a point. The islands were under martial law and it was getting dark; we were running out of time. The dangerous time would double in an hour and triple in two.

Because at sundown, shadowy self-deputized block wardens came swaggering out into the night like roaches, guys with itchy fingers who roamed the streets with old rifles and rusty pistols looking for something to shoot.

For the first time in my life I had bad feelings for Japan, because after they destroyed Pearl Harbor, every Japanese person in Hawaii, U.S. citizen or not, became suspect. We got second looks everywhere we went, hooded eyes watching, wondering. Is this one a spy? That one? What are they planning next? It was crazy.

Mr. Wilson, whose land we lived on, was one of those guys. He was part of an organization called the BMTC, the Businessmen's Military Training Corps. Only white people, haoles, could be in it. And they all had guns. At school, our teacher Mr. Ramos warned us to watch out for them even though we were kids, because sometimes those guys got trigger-happy. "We're in the middle of a war now. It's dangerous, and the future is unknown."

I glanced back at the deckhouse on the *Taiyo Maru,* the only visible part. Too much time had passed. The engine was probably shot. But . . . maybe it could be cleaned up and fixed. The hull would dry out and be fine, but the moving parts were probably crusted with corrosion.

Billy nudged me and motioned with his chin.

Down the way, emerging from the bushes, seven guys broke out and bunched toward us. Haoles. Older than us, maybe by two or three years. I'd seen some of them around but didn't know them by name.

Except for one.

Seeing him was like swallowing gasoline.

Me and Billy slipped into the weeds.

3
RACING SUNDOWN

Back on the streets it was easy to hide.

For sure, the seven white guys didn't know this part of Honolulu like we did, a jungle of alleys and old buildings. Loose-planked fences to escape into. Spooky streets they might worry about going down, streets with mean dogs and centipede boys who wouldn't be happy to see haoles anytime, anywhere, especially rich guys who lived in green neighborhoods up near the mountains, sons of the BMTC who made it clear that they were keeping their eyes on anyone who wasn't like them.

Which meant me.

Billy, too, for that matter. They called him a Jap-loving traitor.

Mr. Davis, Billy's father, told us, "Guys like that are ignorant," as if he were spitting the words. "Ignore them.

14

Don't engage them. You fight with skunks, you always come away smelling bad."

Which was just exactly what Papa would have said if he'd been here. *Don't fight, Tomi-kun,* he would say. *Don't shame the family. Be helpful, be generous, be accepting.* He always said stuff like that, even about people who were anything but those things.

Papa didn't know how hard that was for me.

But my Grampa Joji would fight back. I knew he would—at the right time, and someplace where shame wouldn't be a problem, because no one would see him. Grampa had no second thoughts about standing up for himself.

But Grampa was over seventy years old.

I frowned, thinking back to right after Pearl Harbor got bombed. Fear had made me and Grampa Joji hide everything we had that was Japanese—the *butsudan,* the altar to my grandmother; all Mama's letters from Japan; the photograph of the emperor; Grampa's flag of Japan; and whatever else we had. Most important was our family *katana,* or samurai sword, the symbol of our family's long history. I'd wrapped it in a *furoshiki* scarf and a burlap sack, then buried it in a secret place in the jungle, feeling ashamed that I'd had to do it. I'd thought to ask Billy if he would hide it at his house, but didn't, because if he got caught helping us do that it might get the Davises in trouble.

I mashed my lips together. Just thinking about doing that to Billy's family made me feel ashamed.

After I'd buried the katana I went back into the jungle every few weeks to dig it up and clean it so it wouldn't rust or corrode. Then I'd bury it in a new location in case of . . . I don't know what . . . but it made me feel better. Nothing was as important to our family as that katana, and I would fight to my last breath to guard it. I dreamed of the day when I would dig it up for the last time and shine it until I could see my face in its blade, then display it so it would be the first thing Papa and Grampa would see when they came home.

"Look," Billy said, lifting his chin toward the side of a sorry-looking concrete building freckled with bullet holes. Boards covered its windows, and the front was pockmarked and gouged with shrapnel from the day of the attack. Most of the damage around Honolulu had been done by us, firing back at the Japanese planes. Those bullets had to land somewhere.

We hurried on, racing the sun.

Like seeing the shot-up boat, the pocked building made me think about Papa. Long ago I'd given up hope that the army would figure out that he wasn't siding with Japan and would release him. Now, my only hope was the end of the war. When it was over he'd come home—I would never stop believing that. And when he did, he would need that boat. I couldn't even imagine what his life would be like without it. How would he work? How would we survive? We'd never be able to save enough for another boat.

"Why're you so quiet?" Billy said. "Still thinking about bringing it up?"

"I guess."

"It's too big of a job, Tomi. You'd need heavy equipment."

"Maybe we could get it."

He snorted.

16

"Okay, maybe we can't get heavy equipment, but with enough guys . . . you, me, Mose and Rico. Some of the guys on the team, we could—"

"We're ninth graders, not a salvage operation."

"So?"

"So nothing. We're just talking."

We headed up toward Nu'uanu, where we lived. Billy's house was on the estate next door to the one we lived on. From my house I could barely glimpse his place, a sprawling white house in the trees. Our house was a small shack on the Wilsons' property. We only lived there because Mama was the Wilsons' housekeeper. Mr. Wilson was a banker. They had a big house with a jungly green yard, a tennis court, a dog, Rufus, and one son—an eleventh grader named Keet.

Who was the one who'd sent the gasoline through my gut down at the canal.

We used to be friends, me and him. But around the beginning of sixth grade that easy world caved in and I quickly turned into his worst enemy. I don't know why for sure, but Billy thought he knew. It took me a week to force it out of him. Keet Wilson had been told by his friends at school that white guys weren't supposed to like Japanese guys, so what was he doing hanging around with me?

Fine, I thought. If that was the way it was. Fine.

I could live with that. I didn't need him.

It was too bad, though, because I used to like Keet. I learned things from him. He was smart, very smart. All he had to do was hear something once and he remembered it. He craved anything to do with the military, too. Actually, he was obsessed by it. "You ever heard of Annapolis?" he once said. "Well, that's where I'm going." He told me about the United States Naval Academy, and how you could learn to fly fighters there, and become an officer in the navy after you got out. He had his eye on flying off aircraft carriers. "Wow," I said. "Maybe I'll go to that academy too." He laughed and said, "I don't think so."

Only now did I understand that laugh.

Still, we both liked the idea of being up there in the clouds. For me it was all about Papa's pigeons, and the freedom I felt watching them, white specks circling in the blue sky.

Keet even used to watch them with me.

But that world crumbled long ago. First he just ignored me. Then he told me to stay away from him. Then he got dangerous.

One day in the jungle, he crossed the line.

It was right after Pearl Harbor. Keet started spying on me. He'd been creeping around with his .22 rifle one afternoon and caught me cleaning the buried katana. He pointed the rifle at my chest. "Give me that Jap sword," he said. He wanted it, like the military was confiscating things from Japanese people all over the island, things they thought could be dangerous to the USA. I said something like *Over my dead body,* not afraid of him or his rifle, not when it came to the katana. I was even ready to break my promise to Papa not to fight.

It was just us, alone, face to face.

Lucky for both of us, he backed down. That day I learned something about Keet Wilson that the navy might not like—he gave up easy. Maybe he was afraid to fight. It seemed to me that if you were going to fly off an aircraft carrier into battle you needed all the guts you could find, and then some.

※※※

It was late, darkness now coming down like a hammer.

Billy walked faster, me right behind him, no money left for a bus.

Soon the crush of town faded away, replaced by wide streets and dark yards protected by thick hedges. Quiet, already asleep.

Or maybe ready to jump out of the bushes and start firing.

"You heard anything about your grampa yet?" Billy said.

"Not a peep. Like he fell in a hole somewhere."

"It still doesn't make sense why they arrested him."

"He's just a grumpy old man."

"Maybe they'll let him go, too much trouble."

I laughed. "I'd leave the door unlocked and hope he'd escape in the middle of the night."

"Confonnit," Billy said.

That cracked me up. It was Grampa's favorite word when he couldn't think of anything else to say. It felt good to laugh.

"Look," Billy said, pointing with his chin.

The park wasn't much like it used to be with its wide grassy field to play in, because now it was scarred with trenches deep enough to jump into if the Japanese bombed us again. In the fading light, Billy and I watched three small blond-haired kids racing around in those trenches. You could only see their hair zipping around.

"They got no problems," I said.

"Except, like us, they better get home quick."

A police car pulled up and cruised slowly beside us. Two police looking over. "You boys headed home?"

"Yessir," Billy said.

We kept walking. They kept driving.

The police looked past Billy at me. "Where's your gas mask?"

"Uh . . . home," I said.

They stopped so we did, too.

"Your IDs, both of you," one guy said without getting out of the car.

We dug them out of our pockets. Everyone had one now, and you had to carry it everywhere you went. Your gas mask, too, but they were heavy and ugly and we never took them with us.

The guy checked our IDs, then handed them back. "You boys start carrying your gas masks. You never know when you might need them."

"Yessir," we said at the same time.

The car moved on.

We hurried home in silence, daylight down to a flicker. Soon the light would die . . . and the roaches and block wardens would come out.

4
LITTLE
BRUISER

A dirt path cut through the bushes from the street up to the small green house I lived in with Mama and Kimi. Billy's house was beyond the trees to the left, the Wilsons' above and to the right. Both were hidden from view by a jungle of bushes and tall trees that roared in the wind like the surf.

It was dark now, everything murky. Shadows and shapes. I held out my hand to stop Billy.

"What?" he said, crouching.

"That dumb goat. You see it?"

Billy squinted into the darkness. "No."

We started ahead slowly, eyes on the black spots in the bushes.

A month back Mr. Wilson had bought a pygmy goat and brought it over to our house with a face that meant business.

"Tie this goat up on a long rope," he said. "Let it eat down all these weeds. This place looks like a junkyard."

That was because I couldn't do everything that needed to be done to hold back the jungle. The weeds and vines grew too fast, closing in to swallow our house. The lawn that grew in sad patches in the dirt we called a yard was as tough to cut as old rope. Grampa Joji used to keep it all from swallowing us with a machete and a rusty push mower we had stored under the house. But he had all day to do that. I didn't.

Billy crept behind me. "Maybe it's out back," he whispered.

"He's a bag of tricks. You can't trust that thing."

I'd named the goat Little Bruiser, because my legs were covered with bruises from his attacks. He must have been owned by someone with boys he didn't like, because he never went after Mama or Kimi. Just me and my friends.

The place was still. A relief.

"Tomorrow," Billy said, hurrying over to the trees and the trail to his house.

"Don't forget your gas mask," I whispered.

"Too late. I already forgot it."

"Pfff," I scoffed. For the first few months after Pearl Harbor we carried those bug-face masks everywhere. But then we stopped, like most people did. The cops had to be tired of talking to people about them.

My lazy half-beagle mutt, Lucky, came stretching out from the cool space under the house. One of her pups peeked out from behind her, a smudge in the night—Kimi's puppy, Azuki Bean. And behind Azuki Bean were the two pups I still had to find homes for. It wasn't getting any easier because they were over a year old now.

Lucky lowered her head, acting all shame at getting caught napping, or maybe she was just shaking off a dream. "My scraggly welcoming committee." I squatted down. "Hey, you dogs seen that goat?"

Lucky yawned and nudged my hand with her wet nose.

"That's what I thought," I said, scratching her dusty head. I glanced up.

The shape of Grampa's beat-up, rusty bike sagged against the side of the house. Weeds had grown into its spokes. It hadn't been ridden since the police and FBI took him away.

"Ho!" I screeched, startled out of my skin when Little Bruiser streaked around the side of the house, coming at me as if fired from a cannon. I leaped up. Lucky scurried back under the house. Little Bruiser's rock-hard head nicked my shin, stinging like a Portuguese man-of-war. "Ow!" I hobbled up the steps and slammed through our screen door into the house.

I looked back out at him, staring at me from the top step. "One day I going sell you for dog food!" I rubbed my leg.

Little Bruiser stared me down as if he owned the place and I was the intruder.

"Git! Beat it!"

He didn't budge.

"Confonnit."

I thought, Did I just say confonnit? Jeese, I'm becoming Grampa Joji.

The house was quiet. "Anybody home?"

No answer. It was dark as a cave in our front room. The house was so empty now, with all our Japanese stuff hidden or buried, some of it under the house, some in the jungle.

Something was cooking, filling the house with good smells. I heard voices and the sound of Kimi clomping up the back steps laughing. I headed into the lightless kitchen.

"Tomi-kun," Mama said, following Kimi into the house. Kimi was carrying a small lantern, turned low. You had to have it if you went to the outhouse in the jungle behind the house. That place was a gamble even in full-on daylight.

"Why you so late today?" Mama went on. "Black out the house so we can get some light."

"Hi, Kimi," I said, ruffling her smooth black hair with my hand. Her blue dress looked out of place above her dusty bare feet and weed-scratched legs. "How many eggs did Ojii-chan's chickens make today?"

"Twenty-eight," she said, jumping up and down as if she'd just located all the gold in China.

I knelt down and faced her. "Wow, that's a good haul. You sell some?"

"The store wanted all of them, but we kept four."

"Go, Tomi," Mama said, waving toward the windows.

"Okay, okay."

I stood and rubbed Kimi's head one more time. Her smile made me happy, blue sky peeking through clouds.

Mama worried too much about blacking out the house. But who could blame her? She had a friend downtown whose kitchen light got shot out, right through the window from the street. Some BMTC guy. It was crazy out there.

Some people thought if they could see a light at night, enemy planes could see it too, and come bomb us again. But that didn't make much sense to me, unless the Japanese had a new kind of plane that hung around in the sky like a cloud with nothing to do but wait for small lights to pop on.

But it was the law.

I quickly taped old pieces of cardboard boxes over every window in the kitchen and the front room, where we lit candles at night. Every other room would stay dark.

That night we ate rice, spinach, and eggs by candlelight, huddled quietly at our small kitchen table. I wondered if Kimi and Mama felt as lonely as I did with Papa and Grampa missing. I wanted to talk about them, and about the boat, too, but it would only make Mama worry.

Later, I lay down on a tatami mat with Mama and Kimi to sleep on the floor in the front room where we spent almost every night these days. I'd peeled away the cardboard so we could get some fresh air, the candles pinched out with licked fingers.

Around midnight I was jarred awake by the wail of sirens.

A fire truck, or an ambulance.

The wailing faded off and the island fell silent.

5
GUNS
IN
THE
NIGHT

The sirens wailed again minutes later and kept going.

Overhead, something rumbled in the sky, a lot of something. The sound rolled through the hills, caught in the valley, tumbling down. Planes, flying low—a sound I would never in my life forget, because it chilled me to the bone.

The whole house rattled.

I sprang up, hopping as I dragged my pants on. I ran outside to stand in the inky black night, cocking my head toward the hills.

Planes, for sure.

Fear raced through me, copper swelling on my tongue. My breathing was shallow, like I couldn't get enough air.

They were back.

The Japanese!

Searchlights burst into the sky, crisscrossing beams

searching for the enemy. Big antiaircraft guns down by the ocean boomed to life, shaking the night. The flickering of gunfire reflected off the low clouds that hung over the city and blanketed the mountains beyond.

Boom!

Crummp.

Mad searchlights. Terrifying drone. I held my head, wanting to scream. Big guns boomed. My brain howled: *Run back inside, tell Mama and Kimi to run for cover! Get out of the house and go into the trees!*

But I couldn't move.

I jumped when Mama put her hand on my shoulder. "Come inside, Tomi-kun," she said, almost in a whisper. "Come."

"But—"

"Only planes, Tomi," she said. "They not bombing. Listen."

Mama pulled me close. I listened.

She was right. There was only the distant antiaircraft fire. No bombs, a sound we all knew too well.

Back inside the house I sat next to Kimi, who was trembling under a blanket that completely covered her. I rested my hand on her back, warm to the touch. "It's all right, Kimi. It's going to stop soon."

A few minutes later the navy gunfire fell silent. But sirens still wailed in the far distance, and my heart still raced.

Kimi finally fell asleep, but Mama lay awake. I could tell by the way there was no sound to her breathing.

When I tried to sleep, I saw Japanese soldiers slinking ashore in my crippled dreams.

I saw bombers.

I saw prisoners . . . us . . . wounded and beaten.

When you've been inside a war—standing under falling bombs, breathing the smoke, smelling rubber burning, hearing who has died and seeing the damage all over your once peaceful island—you can't shake it off. They could still come back. It could happen again.

But now we had barbed wire stretched across our beaches, and old trucks and cars parked in the way of any ocean landing, and we had the army sitting in foxholes, and the BMTC, the Hawaii Rifles, Civil Defense, and the VVV, the Varsity Victory Volunteers, who were Japanese American university ROTC cadets dismissed from the program after Pearl Harbor. They wanted to join the army and do their part, but after Japan attacked us no Japanese Americans were allowed to enlist. So they started the VVV and did what they could on their own, mostly building things and stringing barbed wire for the military.

And then there were guys like me and my friends with our BB guns and slingshots stashed in the corners of our closets.

Still, fear had me by the throat.

What saved me that night was Papa's boat. I lay in the dark, thinking: There has to be a way to bring it up, just has to.

Somehow, someway, the *Taiyo Maru* was coming up.

6
SHOT

The next morning, as always, I caught a ride to school with Billy and his parents, me and Billy in the backseat. My whole family liked the Davises. Mrs. Davis was a nurse, blond, as tall as Mr. Davis, and quiet, but strong, too, as Mama described her. She was the kind of person who thought before speaking, then said just exactly what was on her mind. Billy told me she'd been raised in Africa, the only child of two missionary doctors. She was quiet because she spent so much of her life worrying about people who had nothing, and it bothered her that there was very little she or anyone else could do about it, Billy said. But sometimes she'd break out into the loudest laugh you ever heard. It was always a jolt to me.

Mr. Davis grew up on a ranch near Galveston, Texas, and was a big boss down at Matson Shipping. He and Papa often talked about fishing, and boats, and how they were both drawn to a big sky with lots of sun and wide-open spaces. Mr. Davis was kind of skinny and sometimes goofy, with curly brown hair, glasses, and an Adam's apple that made him look like he'd gotten an egg stuck in his throat. Sometimes he went around talking like a cowboy, his accent like a tickle in my ears. It embarrassed Billy but always made me laugh.

I wasn't in the car five seconds before Billy said, "We shot at our own planes last night. Five bombers were flying in from the mainland and got lost over the blacked-out island."

"Ho, really? They were ours?"

"Luckily, none of them got hit."

"We can thank the low clouds we had last night," Mr. Davis said over his shoulder. "It could have been disastrous."

"Spooky," I said.

Mr. Davis turned out onto the street. Mrs. Davis sat with her eyes closed, her freckled elbow out in the breeze. She worked at Queen's Hospital and hardly ever got enough sleep, Billy said. Since Pearl Harbor she'd been working twelve-hour days and was only now starting to cut back.

"They all got down fine," Mr. Davis added. "Just a little shaken up."

"Shook me up too," I mumbled.

We rode in silence after that, heading down the green-hedged street and turning out onto Nu'uanu Avenue near the Piggly Wiggly grocery store. All I could think about was bombs, gunfire, bayonets, and graves.

I looked up when I remembered: my gas mask!

Billy'd forgotten his, too. I made a motion, putting my hand over my face. Billy raised a finger, whispering, "Shhh."

I grinned. At least one thing wasn't so serious.

The whole way over to Roosevelt High School Mrs. Davis slept. Or maybe she was thinking about what could have happened last night if those planes had been hit. More than any of us, she knew about death. She told Billy that when the Japanese bombed Pearl Harbor she'd seen more dead bodies and beat-up people than she ever cared to see again. Enough was enough.

Mr. Davis pulled over in front of the school.

We got out and thumped the door shut.

"Billy," Mrs. Davis said, frowning. "Where's your gas mask?"

"Uhh . . . I forgot it."

She looked at me. "You too, huh?"

I stared at my feet.

"You boys need to start carrying those around again. I know it's safer now, but it's still dangerous."

"Sure, Mom."

Mrs. Davis shook her head.

Billy waved as his dad gave us a thumbs-up and drove off to the hospital, taking the shortest possible route because of gas rationing. Most people only got ten gallons a month.

I glanced up at the school, a red-roofed white building that sat above the street on a grassy rise. The wide slope where we always found our friends Mose and Rico waiting for us was covered with kids . . . but no Mose and no Rico.

"Must have gone in already," Billy said, though it was still early and Mose and Rico, who were cousins, always stalled as long as they could before going into any class-room.

Inside the school we ran into Mr. Ramos, our history teacher—he was also Mose and Rico's uncle. He'd been our science teacher last year, but since some of the men teachers had gone off to war, he was now teaching classes in a few grades. Mose said Mr. Ramos wanted to go help out in the war too, but the principal begged him to stay. They needed him at school, because nobody could work with the boys like he could. He was the best teacher I'd ever had.

"Morning, boys," Mr. Ramos said. "How's things?"

"Good," Billy said.

"Where's Mose and Rico?" I said.

"You didn't hear!"

"Hear what?"

"Rico got shot."

"What!" we both said.

Mr. Ramos put up his hands. "He's okay. But last night he took a twenty-two in his . . . his rear end."

Me and Billy glanced at each other. I felt shaky.

"They were roaming around after dark with their BB guns like they weren't supposed to, and some fool took a shot at them. Actually, it was about five shots, but only one hit. Those boys should have known better than to be out after curfew."

"Who shot at them?" I said.

"One of those guys walks around keeping the curfew or whatever they think they're doing. Listen to me: don't mess around at night, you understand? It's still very dangerous out there, and it will stay that way for a while."

We nodded.

Shot in the *okole*. Ho. It was almost funny, except when you realized that he could have been hit someplace that could have killed him. "Where's Rico now, Mr. Ramos?"

"Oh, he'll be here today. Probably missed his bus. He's walking kind of slow today, I'm sure."

"Yeah . . . well, see you in class."

Mr. Ramos tapped my shoulder, then shook Billy's hand and went on down to his classroom.

Hoo . . . Rico . . . shot in the butt?

Me and Billy walked down the hall, silent as cats . . . then broke out laughing.

7
BROKEN CURFEW

An hour after school started Rico limped in on crutches. His nurse—Mose—followed. The look on Rico's face was so much like a sick dog's I didn't know whether to hold my breath or laugh.

Mr. Ramos waved for Mose and Rico to come up front where Rico could sit with his legs stretched out. Or try to sit.

"Sorry we're late, Uncle," Mose said. "Rico moving kind of slow."

"I see that. Before you sit down, Rico, you want to tell the class what happened to you?"

"No," Rico mumbled.

Mose turned up his palms and shrugged.

Rico switched both crutches to one hand and eased down, wincing. He set the crutches on the floor and sat staring at his hands, pressed flat on his desk.

"He got shot," Mose said.

Everyone in class who didn't know sat stunned.

"In the butt," Mose added, grinning.

"Shuddup." Rico slapped Mose with the back of his hand. "Tst." A few snickers erupted in the back row, but most just sat blank-eyed, probably wondering if it was a joke or what.

"That's right," Mr. Ramos said. "Rico got shot."

The room fell silent.

"Rico took a bullet because he was out after curfew. Some people just have to learn things the hard way, you know?"

He paused in front of Rico's desk.

Rico wouldn't look at him.

Mr. Ramos went on. "But to the rest of you, let me say it again—do *not* go out after dark. It's very, very dangerous. Rico was lucky, and I'm sure he's learned his lesson. But *please,* follow the rules and respect the curfew. These are very unstable times. Okay? Will you do that for me?"

We all nodded, mumbled, sure, sure.

Later that day when school let out, me and Billy walked with Mose and Rico down to the bus stop. All of us went home on the city bus, them one way, me and Billy another.

"So, Rico," I said. "Did it hurt to get shot?"

"Naah. Like a bee sting. It's nothing."

"Pshh," Mose spat. "He cried like a baby."

"You don't shut it up Mose I going remake your face."

"You're lucky the guy only had a twenty-two," Billy said.

"Right about that, brah," Mose said. "If he had a big gun Rico might only have one cheek now."

"Tst," Rico said. "You really starting to burn me up, you know, Mose . . . ah?"

Mose put up his hands in surrender.

"Mr. Wilson shot at me one time," I said. "With a forty-five. But he didn't know it was me. That was at night too."

"A forty-five would blow a big hole in you," Billy said.

"Boom! No more *okole,* ah, Rico?" Mose said, dancing away just as Rico swung a crutch at him.

Mose and Rico's bus came and they got on. We watched Rico in the windows, hopping his way back to the last seat. He waved a crutch at us, and the bus lumbered off, coughing black smoke.

8
CREEPY BLACK HOLE

Back on our street, Billy said, "You know that idea you had about trying to bring up your dad's boat?"

"Yeah."

"I've been thinking about it. It's such a crazy idea it's interesting. I still think it's impossible . . . for us, anyway . . . but forget that for a moment. I was thinking, what would the army have to say about it? I mean, they put it there, right?"

I scowled. "So?"

"So don't you think the first thing you should do is see if . . . well, if you could get in trouble, or something . . . if you messed around with the boat, I mean?" Billy cocked his head. "It would be kind of like breaking someone out of jail, you know?"

That made me smile. "Yeah . . . but I wouldn't want to get shot down before I even started."

"But what if you could get arrested?"

"They wouldn't arrest me for trying to save our own boat."

"You sure about that?"

"No."

Billy thought for a moment. Why'd he have to bring this up? I would just do it, that was all. The army didn't have to know. But I knew he was right. The last thing my family needed was more trouble.

"We could ask Mr. Ramos," Billy said.

I shook my head. "Maybe later. First I want to see if I can even figure out how to do it."

Billy shrugged. "Makes sense. But sooner or later we have to check that out, you know? Maybe even get permission, or something."

"Yeah, I know. But for now I want to keep it quiet."

"Sure. For now."

We walked up the path to my house, the afternoon warm and still. Billy was just saying out loud what had passed through my mind the night before, lying awake: would the military care? I didn't want to ask and to take the chance of bringing the boat back into the army's mind when they seemed to have forgotten about it.

"Hey," Billy said. "You want to come over and see our bomb shelter?"

"You dug another one?"

"No, same one, only now it's different."

"Different how?"

"I'll show you."

What was he up to? I'd already seen his bomb shelter.

I helped him dig it right after Pearl Harbor got bombed, something the military governor had urged everyone to build. Billy's was just a hole in the ground with sandbags and lumber on top. A spooky place—dark, dirty, and stinky as a swamp.

We headed through the trees.

When we broke out onto Billy's vast lawn, his dog, Red, another of Lucky's puppies, came tumbling over to jump all over us. Billy squatted down and knocked Red on his side to rub his belly. "Yeah, that feels good, doesn't it?"

Red's rear leg raked the air as Billy scratched him, the dog's eyes closed to happy slits.

Billy's house lay low against the tall trees beyond, as big as the Wilsons' but spread out on one level, not two. The yard was perfect, the grass cut short and the edges clean, the work of the Davises' gardener, Charlie, who was Grampa Joji's good friend.

Billy's older brother, Jake, was lying on the concrete floor of the garage looking up under a jacked-up black Ford. "Jake got a car?" I said.

"Naw, not him. Dad says he has to earn the money for a car himself. That'll take a while. That one belongs to his friend Mike."

"What's he doing to it?"

Billy shrugged. "Looking at the brakes, I think."

Jake glanced out at us from under the car. Then went back to work. He always had a greasy rag hanging out of his back pocket. In our neighborhood, Jake Davis was the guy for car problems. That's how he should make money to buy a car, I thought. But Jake always fixed things for free.

Behind Billy's house, down a sloping grass yard, the bomb shelter sat belowground, dark and creepy as a grave. Red settled down on the grass to watch us, his tongue jiggling in his panting mouth.

Billy pulled three planks away from the entrance. Five dirt steps dropped down into the lightless pit. "Take a look," he said.

"I'm not going in there."

"Too spooky for you?"

I frowned. "No. You go. I'll follow."

Billy studied the gaping black mouth. "Wait. I'll get my flashlight."

Except for the chatter of a few birds, the yard was silent. Nothing moved, not even in the treetops where a breeze usually blew. Billy's parents were still at work.

Minutes later, Billy came jogging back down the grassy slope with the flashlight. He tossed it to me. "Okay, now you got your light. Go."

"I thought *you* were going first."

"Come on, just go down and take a look, you coward."

I stepped down into the hole and flipped on the flashlight.

"Ahhh!" I gasped, staggering back. I fell and crabbed away backwards on my hands and feet. "You punk! You were going to send me into *that*?"

Stupid Billy was laughing so hard he nearly cried. "I knew you wouldn't get past the second step," he said, wiping tears from his eyes.

"Jeese!" I spat. "You feeding them, or what?"

The bomb shelter was alive with centipedes, the six-inch kind that live in the cracks in the earth and crawl up inside your pants when you water the grass. Rusty-red ugly zillion-leg nightmare monsters that could sting like wasps and haunt your dreams for seventeen days. Or years.

I stood up and turned off the flashlight, tossed it back to Billy. "You fool. You're gonna pay for that."

"Yeah, yeah."

"You right, yeah—when you least expect it."

We slammed the boards back over the pit, closing it off before any of those vampires decided to make a break for daylight.

Billy rubbed the heel of his hand over his wet eyes, still laughing. "I just couldn't resist."

"Yeah, it was fun for you, but—"

Billy's smile vanished.

I looked back over my shoulder.

There they were again. But now there were only three of them, standing stone still at the top of the yard.

Dwight Mason. Chip Perry.

And Keet Wilson.

"Heyyy, fish boy," Keet drawled.

I squinted, my hands on my hips.

Keet grinned and wagged a finger at me. "I've been watching you."

9
THE BMTC

"Here come the creeps," I muttered.

"BMTC punks," Billy added. "Think they might be men."

"Yeah, BMTC punks."

The BMTC was a group of men whose main reason for existing was something so spooky I could hardly believe it. It started up just after Pearl Harbor. Most of the BMTC guys were okay, but some weren't. Billy's dad told him about it, and Billy told me, saying it wasn't such a smart thing to have organized. "Because it approaches vigilantism," Billy's dad said.

"What's that?" I asked.

"Like when people take the law into their own hands."

"Like, make up their own laws?"

"Exactly."

What the BMTC was organized for wasn't to patrol for blackout violations or curfew breakers, like they wanted everybody to think. No, their real mission, the hidden one, was to take care of *enemy aliens* if and when the Japanese returned to invade the islands. Enemy aliens were people like Mama, Papa, and Grampa Joji, who lived here but weren't U.S. citizens. I was born here, so I was a citizen. What did Billy mean by *take care of*? It didn't sound good.

Billy said the BMTC had huge wall maps flagged with areas on the island where there were heavy concentrations of Japanese people. When he'd told me that, a wave of fear broke over me. I thought of Mama alone in our house and how they could come and take her away.

But I also knew our house wouldn't be flagged on anyone's map, because it was on haole property. Still, no matter where I went, I would be on Keet Wilson's map—to him a Jap is a Jap, and Japs crushed Pearl Harbor.

Now he stood at the top of Billy's yard, watching me.

Keet and the two other guys, Dwight and Chip, strolled down the slope. Red leaped and nipped at their legs, looking for attention.

Keet knelt down with one knee cocked and rubbed Red's head. Dwight and Chip stood watching. Keet scratched behind Red's ears, whispering to him. "You're a cute little feller, ain't ya? Yeah."

Keet looked up, still scratching Red's ears. "You traitors got something I should know about hidden in that pit?" When neither of us answered, he stood and walked closer to peer around Billy. Billy was almost as tall as Keet.

Keet waited for an answer. Black hair, blue eyes, clean

face with no zits. Wiry, muscular arms. Fake army dog tags around his neck.

Me and Billy kept silent.

"Oh, my," Keet said to his friends. "Look . . . they're trying to be tough guys."

Dwight snickered.

Chip pushed Red away with his foot. "Git."

"One more time," Keet said. "What's in the pit?"

Billy handed Keet the flashlight. "See for yourself."

Keet took the flashlight, his eyes boring into Billy's.

"No, don't," I said, blocking the boarded entry.

"Move," he said.

The corner of Billy's mouth curled so slightly you could barely see it.

Keet yanked the planks aside and stepped down into the hole. Other than the centipedes, all that was down there were a few boxes of canned food, two chairs, a couple of cots to sit on, and ten gallons of water.

Keet shined the light around. "What's in these box—"

He froze. Centipedes were crawling up his pants and oozing up over his bare feet. He shrieked and came flying out, dropping the flashlight.

"Get them off me!" he screamed, slapping at his pants. *"Ahh! Ahh!"*

Billy and me backed off, trying so hard not to laugh.

Chip and Dwight scurried away, not wanting to get stung.

"They're crawling up my *leg*!" Keet yelled. He ripped off his pants, batting at three centipedes making their way up to his blue and white striped boxers.

I tried to control my face.

He slapped the last one off and glared at us. "You sick animals!"

He searched his pants, then put them back on and lunged toward us, his eyes bulging with rage. He took a swing at me, but I jerked my head back. He swung again, hitting my shoulder. Then Billy was on him. They fell to the grass.

Red started leaping around and yapping, making a terrible racket, thinking it was a game.

Dwight shoved me down, then came at me with his fist cocked. I moved and his knuckles hit grass. Chip went for Billy and grabbed him from behind, holding his arms back. Keet jumped up and was about to drive the hammer of his fist into Billy's face when he saw the Davises' gardener, Charlie, running down the slope with a shovel held up like a baseball bat. Chip let go of Billy and backed off with his hands up. "Dwight," he said.

Dwight looked over his shoulder and rolled off me, stood and backed away.

Charlie tossed me the shovel, grabbed Keet by the back of his pants, and yanked him away from Billy, strong as a bull. "Nuff!" he snapped. "Nobody going beef in my yard!"

Keet tumbled back, then leaped up ready to go at it with Charlie, but he was smart enough to change his mind.

"Go home," Charlie said. "Go back your place."

"You're going to be sorry you stepped into this, old man," Keet spat. "I'm going to get you fired."

Charlie said, "You do that, boy, but for right now you jus' get out of this yard."

"All right, no problem, but I'll be back to watch them kick your sorry self back to the dump you came from."

Charlie glared at him.

Keet came up to me, eyes burning. "I know what you're planning to do with your pappy's boat, fish boy," he growled. "I ain't stupid. But *you* are." He jabbed a finger into my chest.

Charlie put his big hand on Keet's shoulder. "Time to go."

Keet shrugged him off, his eyes still pinned on me. "Get this clear, you so much as touch that boat and I'll get you arrested. This is war, now. You hear me? And you Japs started it, not us. There is no way anyone in his right mind is letting you use that boat against us again, so nail this into your brain: you mess with that boat, you messing with me, because I'm going to take you down. Count on it."

That did it.

The boat was coming up.

10
FRIENDS

A couple of weeks later Rico was limping around school without his crutches. He said his *okole* still hurt, like if you just got a shot in it at the doctor's. He was shuffling like an old man, but he still had his usual stick match in his mouth, a toothpick with a red tip, so I knew he felt better if he was thinking about being cool.

Mose, as usual, had the sleeves of his shirt rolled up to show off his muscles. "We go sit in the shade," he said. "Too hot."

We sat in the dirt, leaning back against the side of the building. Rico winced as he gingerly lowered himself, trying to squint and look tough, which made me laugh. He would do anything to keep from looking sissy. I had to admire him, though. Sitting on a shot-up *okole* was pretty manly.

Funny thing was, I was feeling manly too. Or maybe it

47

was anger. Two things had collided in my mind—Papa's boat and Keet Wilson. It was kind of like when we got bombed. One day you're sitting around minding your own business, and the next you got a war on your hands.

That was me and Keet.

His father never really liked or trusted my family, for some reason, but he pretty much left us alone. But for Keet to threaten me about Papa's boat was going too far, just like he went too far that day in the jungle when he tried to take the katana from me. The more nasty he got, the more stubborn I got. He even made me angry enough to consider breaking my promise to Papa.

Don't fight and shame this family!

I would bring that boat up first for Papa, then for me. To get beaten down by a fool like Keet Wilson was something I could not accept.

If I had to fight, I would fight.

Sorry, Papa.

Don't fight, Papa's words blared in my head. I covered my ears. Then realized where I was and took them away.

Mose, Rico, Billy, and I sat silently for a few minutes, watching the ants crawl in the dirt. Mose was right, it was hot. The back of my shirt was sticking to me.

"Hey, Mose," I said. "How long can you hold your breath?"

"Why? You going fut?"

"No, really. Two minutes? More?"

He shrugged. "Maybe. What you talking about?"

I knocked Billy's arm with the back of my hand. "Me and Billy are going to bring up a sunken boat."

"What?" Billy said.

"My father's sampan. We were hoping you and Rico could help us."

Billy snorted. "I told you, we need heavy equipment, and maybe you forgot to check, but we just don't happen to have any salvage cranes hanging around."

"It's not impossible," I said.

Then I told Mose and Rico what Keet Wilson said—if I mess with the boat, then I'm messing with him. "What would you do? Bow down and say, *Yessir, master sir, you know best, whatever you say, you got it*"?

"That punk like die," Rico said. "Stupit haole."

"He said he'd get me arrested," I added.

"You think he can?"

I shrugged.

"We could arrest him," Rico said, the stick match bouncing in his mouth. "Make our own police force for getting stupits off the streets. Or maybe we could join up with those VVV guys and get them to help us deal with that punk."

Mose frowned at him. "You gotta be Japanese for be one VVV, you idiot."

"For Tomi, I going be Japanese."

"Thanks, Rico," I said.

"Anyway," Billy added, "those VVV guys all joined up with the Four Hundred Forty-second Regimental Combat Team. The army finally let them in."

"No kidding," Rico said. "That's good."

Mose looked at me. "So what's your plan?"

"I don't have one . . . yet."

Billy shook his head.

"After school, we go check out the boat," Mose said, then gave me a toothy grin.

"You're all nuts," Billy said. "You don't know what you're even talking about."

Mose wagged his eyebrows.

Nobody had better friends than me.

11
THE BOAT GRAVEYARD

We took the trail through the trees out to the vast dirt patch. Out in the canal the *Taiyo Maru* and other sampans looked like busted tree stumps in a flood. I imagined carrying a bucket of water, and how heavy it would be. Just one bucket. The *Taiyo Maru* sat under a *million* buckets. Billy was right. We'd need heavy equipment.

But I couldn't give it up. Not now. Not ever. If I did, it would be like letting my small family fall apart, day by day, until there was nothing left but dust where our old life had been.

Stop thinking! I kept telling myself. Just do it, bring it up and make it work again for when Papa comes home, because he *is* coming home. *He is coming home.* And so is Grampa Joji.

I glanced toward Diamond Head, then back over toward

Honolulu. No one else was around, no kids playing in the dirt, no fishermen casting off the rocks for mullet.

"Gee, Tomi," Rico said. "That ain't no small boat. What we can do with only four guys?"

Mose whistled, low. "Billy, your daddy got a crane down his office?"

Billy humphed. "That would do it."

I took off my shirt and pants, down to my white boxer BVDs. "Well . . . no time like now to get started, ah? Mr. Ramos said if you got a lot of homework you take it one bite at a time, like how you would eat an elephant, right?"

"You eat elephants?" Rico said.

Mose laughed and hooked his thumb toward Rico. "He's serious."

Rico scowled.

Billy eased down to sit and watch from the rocks at the edge of the canal. "This I got to see."

"Whatchoo going do, Tomi?" Rico asked.

"First thing I need to know is how the hull is. If it has a big hole in it, then we probably don't have much of a chance to fix it up. But if it only has a small hole, maybe we can."

Mose and Rico joined Billy on the rocks.

"Go," Mose said. "We wait for you."

The warm water had a faint swampy stink. It was brown, but clear enough to see. Just rusty water.

The *Taiyo Maru* was only ten feet from shore. I swam over and stood on the deck, about three feet down. Slimy moss had grown on the wood, making it slippery under my bare feet.

I jumped off and dove under to look for holes in the hull.

It was darker down there; I needed goggles to see. I'd borrow some from Charlie, who had spear-fishing gear.

I came up for air and went down again. It took a while, but I ran my hands over almost every inch of the wood hull. Grampa was right, there was a hole, chopped from the inside out. But it was small. It could be fixed. Probably.

That was good.

Still, this hulk full of water must weigh ten tons. Man, I thought, gliding back to the surface. I was a lunatic to think I had a chance.

12
DEATH WISH

When I popped up, Billy, Mose, and Rico were sitting stone still with Keet Wilson, Chip and Dwight, and three other guys standing around them with sticks in their hands.

I swam over the deck and stood on it.

Keet crossed his arms and studied me, shaking his head slightly. "Help me understand this," he said. "I mean, didn't we talk about not messing around here? We did, right?"

I glared back.

Big man, I thought . . . when you got an army standing behind you.

Probably they were sons of BMTC guys. Where else would Keet find someone to back him up over one Japanese kid like me? They probably all went to his same school. But most guys I knew who went there—like Billy's brother— would never allow themselves to be dragged into something like this. Or else maybe these guys didn't go there and just liked trouble. A guy with Keet's brains could tell them anything and they'd believe it. Funny how he could be so smart and so dumb at the same time.

"You come on up out of that water," Keet said, leaning on his stick, which was a jagged, snapped-off tree branch. "We aren't going to let you do this. You must know that by now. Right?"

I stayed where I was.

Keet tapped his thumb on the end of the stick. The smaller limbs were sharpened to points.

Mose stood and stretched, as if nothing were behind him but the sun and a few lazy flies. He yawned, then took off his shirt and pants and, in his BVDs, jumped into the water. "Where do we start?" he said, swimming out to me.

Keet's eyes narrowed.

Then Rico creaked up.

Then Billy.

Keet shoved Billy from behind. "You Jap-loving traitor."

Billy and Rico jumped into the water with their clothes on, swam out to the boat. I grinned at Keet. I shouldn't have, but I couldn't help it.

Keet spat and stabbed his stick into my pants, then beat them into the dirt. He grabbed up our shirts and pants and tossed them into the water.

His six boy-soldiers stood motionless behind him, smirking.

Slowly, they all backed off and left, Keet mumbling something at us. As scared as I was of them, they weren't what I was thinking about.

"Rico, get out! This could be sewer water. It could infect your wound. Clean it good when you get home."

"What wound?" he said.

But we all got out and pulled on our wet clothes.

Sundown had colored the sky red.

Time to get home.

13
A
SHOCK
IN THE
NIGHT

On a Friday night a couple of weeks later, I was awakened by someone whispering my name outside our screen door. I checked the clock in the murky light: 10:30, a half hour past military curfew.

"Tomi."

Billy? I got up and crept toward the door.

Mama was stirring, trying not to disturb Kimi, asleep on the floor nearby. Ever since blackout started over a year ago, we'd lived in that one room and the kitchen, though sometimes I slept in my room.

"Who is it, Tomi?" Mama said.

I squinted into the night through our screen door. "Who's there?"

"It's me—Billy. You got to come with me, Tomi—all of you."

I could barely make him out, standing just beyond where the goat's rope could stretch. Little Bruiser was planted a foot in front of him, barring his way. A shadow in a shadow. On a moonless night in this blackout, the islands were as dark as tar. "We can't go out now. It's curfew."

"We found your grandfather!"

I froze, stunned. "Grampa?"

Behind me Mama gasped. I could hear her scrambling to her feet. "Billy-kun," Mama called. "Come inside."

"I can't," he said. "The goat."

Mama went out on the porch and called into the night. "Shoo!"

The goat trotted off. Billy sprinted across the yard and up the steps. I held the door open. He burst in and stood just inside.

"You . . . you found Grampa Joji?" I managed to say. "You mean you found where they took him on the mainland?"

"No, he's here, Tomi. He's at Queen's. They had him at a stockade on Kauai. He had a stroke. They couldn't care for him there, so they sent him over by boat. My mom saw him come in. He was covered with mosquito bites."

Grampa? *Here?*

"Queen's Hospital?" I said.

"Yeah, where my mom works."

"Oh, no, no," Mama said. "Another stroke."

"Mom says he's not too bad," Billy said. "He can talk, and he recognized her."

"They're letting him stay there?" I said. "Are they going to send him back? Is he under guard?"

58

"Slow down," Billy said. "You can see for yourself. That's why I'm here."

"What do you mean?"

"Mom can get you in to see him."

"Mama?" Kimi said, waking up.

"S'okay, Kimi. We just talking to Billy." Mama bumped through the dark to the kitchen. "Billy-kun, you wait. I go get you some *musubi* to take to him."

"No, Mrs. Nakaji. I'm supposed to bring you to my house, all three of you. Dad's going to drive us to Queen's so you can see him. Don't worry about curfew. You'll be with us. Mom is waiting at the hospital."

"Oh, oh," Mama sputtered. "Tomi, get Kimi ready."

She hurried to her bedroom to change.

"Tomi," Billy said. "Listen!"

My mind was racing. Grampa was here! My *ojii-chan.* Alive, and not on the mainland.

"*Listen* to me," Billy said, shaking my shoulder. "Dad thinks he can get him released."

My eyes locked on his.

"Bring him home, Tomi. Dad thinks we can bring him home."

14
QUEEN'S

Riding to the hospital sometime near midnight in a totally blacked-out town was eerie. Mr. Davis had to crawl through the streets with headlights covered with black tape, and only one small crack of blue to show the road ahead. It was the law.

Billy sat up front with Mr. Davis.

Kimi sat between me and Mama in the back. I wondered if Mama might be holding her breath like I was, unable to think about anything but Grampa, hoping it was really true. We were going to see *Ojii-chan!*

We parked and got out at Queen's. Huge monkeypod trees loomed in the starlight, and beyond, the black mass of the hospital pricked with small red lights. Mama hesitated, staring up at the massive building. She'd never been in a hospital.

"It's okay, Hideko," Mr. Davis said, gently taking Mama's arm. "Come with me."

Mama nodded, and we went in.

Seeing Mr. Davis put Mama at ease like that made me like him even more.

No police or soldiers stood guard outside the door to Grampa's room, like I'd expected. Inside we found a small old man lost in bright-white sheets in a four-bed hospital room. One low light lit the room, the windows covered over with black paper. He was alone, the other three beds empty.

"Grampa!" Kimi cried, and ran over to him.

The rest of us inched in and stood in a clump at the foot of the bed. My breath caught when I saw him. It had been over a year. He looked shrunken, or maybe the bed just made it seem that way. He appeared to be asleep, white lotion spotting a zillion mosquito bites on his face and arms. A frown crept across Mr. Davis's face. "They never should have taken him away from home," he said softly.

Grampa stirred, then squinted one eye open.

Then the other. His mouth curved up when he recognized Kimi.

She grabbed his hand.

"Unnh," he mumbled. "You more big."

Kimi leaned down and rested her head on his shoulder. He patted her back.

I glanced at his ropy mosquito-ravaged brown arm lying on the clean white sheet. Once that arm had been like steel. I could almost feel again the unbearable pain that he could inflict on me by grabbing my wrist and twisting it in a special way—just so—and sending me to my knees. He was the bone crusher. I'd practiced that grip myself, over and over, until I'd gotten it down as good as that old coot.

"Now, now, give the poor man some breathing room," Mrs. Davis said, rushing in. She put her hand on Mr. Davis's arm, smiling across the bed at Kimi.

Mrs. Davis looked up at Mama. "This is certainly our lucky day, isn't it? They could have taken him anywhere, even to another ward in this hospital, and we might have never known he was here." She grabbed Mama's hand. "How are you holding up, Hideko?"

"We are so . . . grateful . . . Mrs. Davis."

"Please call me Marie. Now let's see how Mr. Joji is doing. He's been kind of ornery, you know."

Ho, the relief! If Ojii-chan was well enough to be cranky, he was doing just fine.

"Let's get you a drink of water," Mrs. Davis said, easing her arm behind Grampa's shoulders to help him sit. She took a cup from his bedside table and filled it halfway from a container by the bed.

Grampa slurped it down grudgingly. Some of it dripped off his chin onto the sheet. He lay back down.

"He's better than those mosquito bites make him look," Mrs. Davis said. "He had a small stroke that left him dizzy and gave him some disturbing but temporary vision blurriness. Now he needs rest more than anything. Lots of it, actually, and hopefully you can see he gets that at home."

"Home?" Mama said.

"I'm seeing if I can get him released to my custody," Mrs. Davis said, gazing at Grampa. "Sending this tired old man back to that . . . to that *place* wouldn't do anyone any good, including the military. They aren't set up to be a hospital."

Grampa scowled, then grunted. "Unnnh."

I looked at the polished tile floor, my throat starting to burn. I was so happy to hear that familiar grunt that I wanted to hug him. He'd be horrified, but so what?

"Grampa!" Kimi lifted her head off his shoulder. "The chickens are laying lots of eggs, you should see."

"Unnh."

Mama moved closer and patted his hand.

Grampa tried to sit up but couldn't. "Confonnit," he said, kind of squeakily.

Mr. Davis chuckled.

"Can we really take him home?" I said.

"In a few days, I hope," Mrs. Davis said. "If Mr. Davis and I can clear it."

She adjusted the bedsheets and helped Grampa sip more water. "Dr. Graner said the stroke, though worrisome, was not all that bad. The important thing is to keep him from getting overly excited about things, keep him on an even keel, so to speak." She grinned. "A pretty tall order, huh?" She rested her hand on my shoulder. "And you'll have to help him get some moderate exercise."

Grampa mumbled under his breath. He was groggy, but he understood everything. I could tell by the cocky tilt of his head and the old rascally eyes glaring back at me.

I reached out and placed my hand on his bony shoulder. "It's good to have you home, Ojii-chan."

He didn't even try to slap my hand away.

15
NEVER
SAY
NEVER

A week later, Grampa Joji had improved a lot and was getting well enough to come home soon. He could get out of bed on his own and walk up and down the hallway outside his room. When I took his arm he felt like a flamingo, skinny and bony light. I'd been back to the hospital twice after school to walk with him. He was so cranky I was beginning to think he'd been faking the stroke thing.

But that just made me smile. Being with him, even in the stark, greenish hospital room, made me feel like I was almost complete again after so long. Everything felt different with him back. As much as we grumbled at each other, Grampa Joji was a rock in my life, and I'd missed him almost as much as I missed Papa. When Kimi came with me, Grampa's eyes seemed to get extra watery. Mama always sat near his bed with her hands in her lap, smiling. It was almost like in the before time.

Almost.

***

Saturday.

"What you got?" I said.

Billy lifted the tools he'd dug up in his garage. "Heavy wrench I borrowed off Jake, two screwdrivers, and these," he said, turning around so I could see the four bamboo goggles hanging from his back pocket. "I borrowed them from Charlie."

"Perfect," I said, snapping my fingers. "This is what I got." I swung up the old crowbar we had lying around under our house, but I would only use that if I absolutely had to. "All I could find."

"Not much, is it?"

"Good enough to start with, I guess. Maybe Mose and Rico will bring something."

"Let's go take a look."

We headed toward the street. "How's your grampa doing?" Billy asked.

"That old faker," I said. "Grumpy, impatient, snappy. Same fun-loving guy you knew from before."

"That's good news!"

"Yeah, we can't wait to get him home again."

"Back out with his chickens."

"You watch, first thing he'll do is take Kimi out to check for eggs."

66

Billy chuckled. "Next thing you know he'll be having you take eggs up to the Wilson house again."

"Never."

"I guess we'll see about that, huh?"

"Won't happen. Ever. Going be nothing for you to see."

"Never say never, they say."

"Yeah, well, whoever said that doesn't know the Wilsons."

"True."

We headed down to the bus stop to catch a ride to the canal. Mose and Rico said they'd meet us there. Today we were going to try to remove some boat parts to keep them from getting ruined in the water.

"I still don't think this will work," Billy said.

I grinned. "Giving up already?"

"I'm just saying this is a job for a crane, not a wrench and a rusty crowbar."

"Maybe."

Mose and Rico did bring a couple of tools . . . and, amazingly, two guys from our old baseball team, the Rats. Tough Boy Ferris and Randy Chock came walking up cool as can be. Mose and Rico had run into them on the way to the canal. They went to a different school now, so we hardly ever saw them anymore. All those baseball games were just a memory.

"Heyyy!" I said. "Howzit?"

They grinned. We shook hands.

"Mose and Rico said come help you take this sunken tub apart," Tough Boy said. "They gave me this," he added, lifting a sledgehammer.

"And these," Randy said.

"Baseball bats?"

Mose shrugged.

"The idea is to *bring* that boat up, not smash it up."

Tough Boy frowned. "Aw, man, I thought we was going bus' um up. Would be more fun, ah?" The morning sun gleamed in his brown eyes.

"What we really brought those bats for is for your friend," Rico said. "Him and those punks, they show up again."

"Let's hope they don't."

"No," Mose said, taking a bat from Randy. "Let's hope they do."

Billy, Tough Boy, and I put on bamboo goggles and went down first. Rico's wound, luckily, hadn't gotten infected from his jump into the dirty water. Today I told him, "Stay out. We'll hand you stuff and you can pile it up somewhere."

"Fine," he said. "But you need me, you say so, ah?"

"You got it."

I was glad to have those bamboo goggles, even though they were the old-style Japanese kind. The water was murky. We needed all the help we could get.

Since it was impossible for us to get the engine out, we concentrated on the easy parts, anything to lighten the load, whatever we could take out or off.

We removed the tiller arm, the canvas tarp Papa sometimes used for shade, and a bucket of lead weights. Rico set them out in the dirt and weeds to dry out. A bite at a time, I kept thinking, a bite at a time.

Speaking of bites, it was two o'clock and I was starving.

"Anybody bring food?" I said.

We glanced at each other.

"How's about water?"

Nobody. How dumb was that? I thought, shaking my head. For sure, I wouldn't forget next time, but for now we had empty hands and empty stomachs.

We searched our soggy pockets and between us came up with one dollar and forty-two cents.

"Rico," Mose said. "Try see what you can buy with this. Go the Chinese store up McCully. You know the one?"

"What should I get?"

"T-bone steak," Tough Boy said.

Rico grinned. "You like that well done?"

"Raw, like a man."

"Pfff," Rico said. He headed toward the street.

Halfway across the field, he stopped.

Right on time, I thought, sighing. This was getting old.

Mose, Tough Boy, and Randy picked up the bats.

16
SHAMED

"How come those punks always know when we're here?" Mose said. "Spying on us, or what?"

"Let um come," Tough Boy said. "They can spy this bat up close."

There were nine of them this time, Keet striding like a rooster out in front with that same sharpened stick. His eyes were pinched. Birds pecking in the dirt rose and flew off in his path.

No matter how tough Mose and Tough Boy talked, if things got ugly, we'd be the ones getting hurt, not those nine guys. So far Keet Wilson was pretty much all talk. But now he had bigger backup.

They spread out, silent.

Keet stopped about five feet out. He looked at me.

No way would I speak first.

Finally, he said, "You never did listen. Neither does your mama. I tell her how to make my bed and she always does it wrong. Must be something messed up about you people . . . some part of your brains missing?"

Rico snapped. "Beat it, haole, before I broke your face. You starting to make me mad."

Keet's grin vanished.

His army closed in.

Keet flinched when Mose tossed Rico a bat, his eyes never straying off Keet's.

"Pssh," Rico spat. "Scared, ah, you? How's about you and me go man to man? Ah? What you say? Just us two. Come on, we go."

Keet shoved Rico.

"Wait, wait, wait," Billy said, stepping between them. "This is stupid."

Keet spat on Rico's foot.

Rico pulled the bat back to take a swing at Keet's head.

Every club, stick, and baseball bat flew up, ready.

"Stop!" Billy shouted. "Just hold on."

Nobody moved. In the distance a siren wailed, but not for us.

"Why get everybody into this?" Billy said. "Let Keet and Rico go at it alone, like Rico said. Man-to-man, with no weapons. No need for all of us to fight."

Still, nobody moved. You could almost hear minds grinding that up—man-to-man, settle it that way.

Slowly, bats and clubs came down.

Eyes shifted to Keet.

Inside, I grinned: Keet was scared. Looking at Rico, I would be too.

Rico tossed his bat away. "Now we talking. Come at me, you haole pig." He circled out, motioning Keet closer with his fingers.

Keet's face flushed and the veins on his neck popped out like worms. His eyes searched for a way out. Rico could look insane when he got mad. Like now.

"Come on," Rico said. "I waiting, piggy. Let's go."

Keet swung. He had no choice. It was fight or be shamed.

Rico jerked his head back and Keet missed by a mile.

But Rico didn't.

Bok!

Keet staggered back into the guy behind him.

The guy stood him up and pushed him back toward Rico.

Rico cracked him again.

Flesh slapping on flesh, an ugly sound.

I almost felt bad for Keet.

Keet stumbled up, blood drooling from his nose. He looked at me, not Rico, with hate. He swiped the back of his hand over his lips, coming away with blood.

Dwight grabbed Keet's arm. "Finish this later." He pulled Keet back. Keet made a feeble show of trying to shake Dwight off, but he let Dwight pull him away.

"He's not worth it, Wilson," Dwight said. "You could hurt the little spit, and you don't want to get his mommy all upset, now, do you?"

Rico lunged at Dwight, but Keet tripped him and Rico went sprawling in the dirt. He scrambled back up.

Mose grabbed him from behind. "Let it go, cousin."

Keet and his punks backed away, then turned and headed for the street. I wondered if some of them even knew why they'd come down to the canal.

Dwight stopped and called back. "Don't think this is over. Don't think you're getting out of this, because you're not. Understand, monkeys? Huh?"

He smiled, as if he were nice enough to be somebody's friend. "Bye now."

17
MIRACLE WORKERS

I knew for a fact that today would be the first time ever in his seventy-four years that Grampa Joji had gotten into a car like the Davises', maybe even into *any* car. Trucks, maybe, but never a shiny car that Jake kept purring like a cat.

Kimi, Mama, Billy, me, Jake, and Charlie all stood around talking low in Billy's yard when Mr. Davis drove up the long driveway, slow and importantly, giving Grampa Joji the royal treatment. Kimi jumped up and down with her hands flying in delight, ready to race up the second he got out. Mama held her back.

Mr. Davis parked and went around to help Grampa out.

Grampa creaked up, all five feet three inches of him, and stood straight and tall as he could, like some king. No smile, and no acknowledgment of us standing there holding our breath.

"Unnh," he grunted, then bowed to Mr. Davis.

Mr. Davis bowed back and opened an arm toward us. "They've been waiting for you."

Grampa lifted his chin higher, checking us over. He gave Charlie a thumbs-up, which made Charlie grin. And he nodded politely to Mama. When he saw Kimi, he actually gave her something you could think of as a smile. He held out a hand.

Mama let Kimi go and she ran over and wrapped herself around Ojii-chan's legs. He took her hand. "We go look those eggs," he said, slowly shuffling off with her, heading through the trees to his chicken coops as if he'd never been gone.

I punched Billy's arm. "I told you so."

We cracked up.

"Kimi," I called. "Warn him about the goat." She wouldn't have thought of that, because Little Bruiser left her alone. It was only guys that beast attacked. All we needed was for Little Bruiser to chase Grampa Joji and scare him into another dizzy spell.

Kimi nodded.

"Thank you, Mr. Davis-sama, thank you," Mama said, bowing again and again. Then she hugged him, something she'd never, ever done before to any haole. "Thank you," she said again, backing away and lowering her eyes, her face flushed.

I stood stunned. But in these times anything could happen.

"You're welcome," Mr. Davis said. "And call me John."

Mama hurried after Grampa and Kimi.

I shook my head. That's my grampa. Just go off, like nobody else is here.

Billy glanced at me, grinning. I knew he was thinking the same thing.

Charlie put his hand on my shoulder. "You folks need anything, you come get me, okay?"

"Thanks, Charlie."

"It's great to have him home," Mr. Davis said.

I grabbed Mr. Davis's hand in both of mine and shook it again and again. "Thank you, Mr. Davis, thank you, *thank you*!"

I ran off after Mama, thinking about that goat.

Little Bruiser was right there by the chickens with his legs planted, head slightly down, staring at Grampa. "Watch out," I called. "When he stares like that you know he's going to charge."

Grampa Joji stared back at Little Bruiser.

The goat kept his eyes fixed on Grampa, his head swaying slightly.

Any second now, I thought, trying to get between them.

Little Bruiser and Grampa stood there checking each other out. A moment passed, then the goat loped off to chew on a piece of wood.

What did I just see? Two old goats coming to a mutual understanding to leave each other alone?

Well, good grief.

That night we sat around the table in the blacked-out kitchen, me and Mama on one side and Kimi leaning up against Grampa across from us. Tea steamed from three cups. Mama had cooked him her best hot *udon*, which he slurped up like a thirsty dog.

"So, Ojii-chan," I said, then waited for him to look up.

He just gazed at his steaming teacup. But he wasn't dismissing me with one of his annoyed looks. That was good.

"So," I went on. "What was it like at that camp? Where was it?"

He frowned, and his eyes flicked up and touched mine, for a second. "Kauai," he said. "Wet . . . mosquitoes . . . *plenny* mosquitoes . . . mud all over."

"How . . . how'd they treat you? Good or what?"

He thought, then shrugged. "No problem."

"They treated you okay, then?"

"Jus' those mosquitoes . . . bad, those buggahs, confonnit. Bad food, too. No more squid." He half grinned, then replaced it with his usual frown.

"Did you see anybody you know there? So many people from Honolulu got taken away. I thought—"

He shook his head. "Nuff . . . talk something else now."

"Okay, Ojii-chan, fine. I understand."

I glanced at Mama, who sat with both hands around her teacup. She was probably thinking what I was thinking: if they treated Grampa okay, then they were probably treating Papa okay too.

"Ojii-chan, wait!" I said, suddenly remembering the two postcards we'd gotten from Papa. I'd stuck them between the pages of one of our few books. The first one had come not long after he was arrested. All it said was that he was okay and that he wanted me to take care of things while he was away. Then there were months of silence. I figured the army probably wasn't letting a lot of mail go out of the camps. Anyway, Papa couldn't read or write English.

But a second card arrived a year later, and it made Mama

fall onto the couch and cry—not because of what it said, but because it proved Papa was all right. Like the first card, its postmark had been blackened by a censor.

"We got this one about three months ago, Ojii-chan," I said. "Listen!"

> To my family:
>
> My good friend Dr. Watanabe is writing this for me. He was a dentist in Long Beach, California, before he came here. He has a wife and one son, nineteen years old. Last week the U.S. Army came to the camp looking for volunteers to fight in the war. They have formed an all-Japanese unit. Some of our young men refused to go. They are still angry about having been arrested and imprisoned. But Mr. Watanabe's son was quick to join. These were his parting words to his family: "If I don't prove that I am innocent, then I will always be thought of as guilty, and I am not guilty. I am an American." We were all sad and proud when he and seventeen other boys left the camp. Tomi, I am telling this for you. Have courage like Mr. Watanabe's son. Stand tall and strong for our family. I think of you, Mama, Kimi, and Grampa every day.
>
> Nakaji Taro

Grampa said nothing. He took the card from me and studied the small, neat handwriting, then handed it back, nodding to himself. He pointed toward the first card we'd gotten, and I read that to him, too.

Ojii-chan scowled. "He doesn't know about his pigeons," he said in Japanese.

"No," I said.

Ojii-chan grunted and finished his tca, then went to bed.

***

That night I slept in my room for the first time in weeks. And Grampa slept across from me, happy to be back on his tatami mat. The sound of his ragged snoring was so much like it was in the before time that I fell asleep smiling.

18
THE
NEWSPAPER

Our school, Roosevelt, went from grade seven to twelve, a public school. Keet Wilson and most of those fools he found to back him up went to Punahou, a private school. Billy's brother, Jake, went there too. It was probably the best school in the territory, but not everyone could go there because you had to pay for it.

Our school was open to anyone—sort of.

There were restrictions. You had to pass a test to get in, an oral language test. That meant you had to be able to speak Standard English, as they called it. Anyone who wasn't haole usually had a hard time, because that meant haole English. Most of us grew up with other languages spoken in our homes—Japanese, Chinese, Hawaiian, Filipino, Portuguese—and because of those different languages we all spoke what was called pidgin English so we could understand each other. Pidgin was mangled and twisted with strange words and strange pronunciations from all those other languages. I loved it.

But Roosevelt didn't.

Some of us could turn it off and on like a light switch. Standard English, pidgin English. No problem.

He's such a troublemaker. Or *Ho, da kolohe, him.*

Let's take the bus down to the canal. Or *We go canal.*

Those of us who made it into Roosevelt were lucky for one big reason—the teachers. They cared about us, worked us hard, treated us as if we were important to them. And the best teacher of all was Mr. Ramos, who we sometimes called Mr. Uncle Ramos, because he was Mose and Rico's uncle.

Still, there were some junk teachers too.

One time a teacher whispered to me, "You don't belong here, you know that, don't you?" I wondered if she'd said that to the seven other Japanese kids in my class. But I shrugged it off, remembering something Papa and Grampa Joji taught me: *Gaman,* they'd both say. *Persevere. Face forward. Take that next step, no matter what. Keep going.* Yeah . . . forget the fools.

In Mr. Ramos's class nobody was any better or any worse than anyone else.

"Who can tell me what's going on in the war today?" he asked one day, strolling back and forth in front of the class with his arms crossed.

Nobody raised a hand.

"What?" he said, raising his eyebrows. "Nobody read the paper today? What have I told you about the news-paper, class?"

After a moment of silence, Rico said, "To read it."

"How often?"

"Every day."

"Right. So who read this morning's paper? Or at least glanced at it? What was the headline?"

Silence.

Mr. Ramos faced us. "You folks mean to tell me that my newspaper lecture went in one ear and out the other?"

We all looked anywhere but at Mr. Ramos. Including me. Sometimes I glanced at the paper, but the news was always old, because the only paper we got was the one that Mama saved and brought home from the Wilsons' house after they threw it away.

" 'The Fighting Traditions of the United States,' " Billy said, finally. "That was one headline."

Mr. Ramos took the paper off his desk and held it up. " 'The Fighting Traditions of the United States.' Thank you, Mr. Davis, for taking something important from my class and using it in your life."

He studied us.

"Listen," he said. "This is important. I'll teach you about science, math, geography, or law, if you like, because that's why I'm here. But what I *want* to teach you, more than anything else, is how to be intelligent, alert, aware, and contributing members of the world around you. What I can't accept is to see any of you wandering aimlessly through life, turning whichever way the wind blows and adding nothing to the good in the world. I want your eyes open and your hearts and minds engaged, does that make sense to you?"

We mumbled that it did.

It made perfect sense. But who got up in the morning, foggy and grumpy, and said, *Open your eyes, engage your brain*?

"Listen," Mr. Ramos went on. "The most basic thing you can do for yourself is keep yourself informed." He paused, took a step toward me. "Tomi, do you remember last year, what I said power was all about?"

"Knowledge."

"Right. Knowledge is power. What does that mean, Rico?"

Rico snapped up. "Huh? Oh . . . uh . . . it means if . . . it means if . . ."

"It means if you don't know things, then other people can fool you," Mose said. "Like you can fool Rico because he don't know nothing."

The class laughed, even Mr. Ramos.

Rico eyed Mose, whispering, "You wait."

Mose wagged his eyebrows.

Margaret, a girl across the aisle from me, said, "Knowledge is power because when you know what's going on, you have the best chance to make the right choice when you're faced with a decision."

Mr. Ramos opened his eyes wide. He pointed to Margaret, nodding.

Margaret sank down into her seat, looking embarrassed. She was usually as quiet as an ant.

"Here," Mr. Ramos said, picking up his newspaper and walking over to her. He handed her the paper. "Take a moment to read the lead article, the one about the fighting traditions of the United States. When you're done, tell us in one sentence what it's all about."

Margaret took the paper. She sat straight in her seat.

I tried to sit straighter too, look smarter.

Margaret looked up when she was done. "One sentence?"

"One sentence," Mr. Ramos said.

"But it says a lot of things."

"What did it say that was most important to you? What stood out most?"

Margaret thought. "Okay . . . we fight and keep on fighting, because we have a very important reason to, and that reason is that we love freedom and don't ever want to lose it."

Mr. Ramos looked at the rest of us. "You think this is important to know?"

We mumbled yes.

"Why?"

After a moment of fidgeting, Rico said, "So we know our guys not dying for something stupid."

Mr. Ramos grinned at Rico, then looked at the rest of us. "Read the paper! Now, let's have your homework—you did do *that,* right?"

I made a vow: I would keep on fighting too. I would fight for Papa's boat and for my family, because like freedom, they were the most important things in my life. *Gaman.* Keep going.

19
FUMI

When I got home after school I found Grampa Joji standing in our yard with his arm on the shoulder of a wrinkled old Japanese lady with hair that stuck out like she forgot to brush it.

Mama and Kimi had to be gone, because if they were home, they'd be standing out here with their mouths hanging open just like I was.

I inched closer, keeping an eye on Little Bruiser, straining at the end of his rope.

"This is Fumi," Grampa Joji said.

"Fumi?"

"New frien' I met downtown."

"You must be Tomi," she said. "I heard you strong."

I glanced at Grampa.

"That's what this old man told me."

Grampa grunted.

"He said you could pull up a hundret-fifty-pound fish from you daddy's boat, got a grip like steel."

"Uh . . ."

Grampa was . . . bragging about *me*?

Fumi looked about Grampa's age, but her eyes sparkled like brand-new. She gave me a very un-Japanese hug, her wild hair smelling sweet, like plumerias.

Grampa Joji and Fumi wandered out toward the chickens.

I stood there gawking. Ojii-chan has a girlfriend?

***

"Where is she now?" Mama asked when she and Kimi came home a little after that.

"They went up by the chickens."

Mama shook her head. "They gone. We just came from there."

Kimi held up four eggs, expertly, two in each hand. She set them on the counter by the sink.

"She was old like him, but nicer . . . way nicer. Her name was Fumi."

"Fumi? I don't know any Fumi."

"She was . . . different," I said.

"Like how?"

"Kind of wild looking."

Mama frowned.

"But she smelled good."

Mama's mouth turned up on one side, a half grin. "That old man."

20
THE
KEY

On Saturday, Billy, me, Mose, and Rico went down to work on the boat. This time we wore shorts and brought the four goggles so we could all go in the water. Rico's wound had healed up good.

"You think that punk live by you going come back today?" Rico said. "Because if he is, I got something for him."

"Maybe," I said. "What you got?"

"This." He held up a fist. "I going introduce him to the four brothers."

I chuckled and shook my head.

We removed easy parts from the *Taiyo Maru* and dried them out in the sun. Later, we'd take it all over to the hiding place we'd made in the weeds and trees out near the street. All the stuff we'd removed was hidden there now, with rubbish piled over it to hide the parts even better.

The work was easy so far. But soon we'd have to face getting the hull off the muddy bottom.

"Pfff," I whispered to myself. "How?"

"I going start dragging this stuff over to the bushes," Mose said. "Rico, help me, ah?"

"You got it."

They climbed dripping out of the water.

Billy and I dove down into the bilge. I took out what I found down there—coiled ropes, buckets, a pair of soggy old pants.

Soggy old pants?

Papa's?

My stomach surged, then tightened. Were they his?

I stood chest deep on the sunken deck of the *Taiyo Maru*, the same deck Papa and Sanji stood on the day they got shot, and while they were getting shot, inside the boat, in the hold, were these pants. They hadn't moved since that day. I felt my eyes swell and turned away, fighting back the emotion.

"What'd you find?" Billy said, popping up out of the hold with another coil of rope.

"Just . . . just pants."

Billy understood instantly. "Sorry," he whispered.

I checked the pockets, hoping to find something of Papa's. Anything.

But what I found was a key. I held it up.

"I know what that is," Billy said, "and those aren't your dad's pants, they're Sanji's. That's the key to his truck."

"His truck?" I said, a new realization forming. "His truck!"

We looked at each other. Memories bloomed in my mind—Sanji's smiling face; Sanji scrubbing the deck; Sanji looking at the moon through Billy's binoculars; Sanji pulling up tuna, and joking about me with Papa: "How long you t'ink it going take before this shrimp got any meat on his bones, boss?"

Riding in Sanji's stinky old truck, him with his elbow out the window, whistling as he drove. I rubbed my palm over my eyes.

"What happened to it?" Billy said.

"I don't know," I said, trying to shake the emotion. "I wonder . . . what if . . . what if it's still there at the harbor? Under the trees where he always parked it."

"Somebody had to have come for it," Billy said. "Like his wife."

"She doesn't drive, or at least she didn't before."

I squeezed the key into my palm so tight it left ridges in my skin. "We have to go to the harbor."

Billy nodded. Then shook his head. "It's got to be gone by now. I mean, that was over a year ago."

"Hey!" Mose shouted from way over by the trees.

I stuffed the key in my pocket and looked up. "What?"

"Come here. You'll want to see this."

Me and Billy swam to shore and dropped the goggles onto the dirt.

Mose stood waist-deep in the weeds of our hiding place,

hands on his hips. Rico crouched down. The hatch cover he and Mose had just dragged over was all that was there. Every part we'd removed before was gone.

"Somebody stole everything," Mose said. "The tiller, the lead weights, the ropes and buckets . . . all of it."

No, no, no! This was a disaster.

"I bet I know who took it," Billy said.

Mose spat.

Keet Wilson. Had to be.

"Man, he going had it, now," Rico said.

If Keet took it what could I do? Not one thing. My mother worked for his mother. We lived in a house they owned. If I accused him of stealing, he would make such a stink he'd get Mama fired and we'd get kicked out of our home.

"Call the cops," Billy said. "Stealing is stealing."

"No," I said, "we can't call anyone."

Mose groaned. "Come on, Tomi, you can't just do nothing."

"We live on his land, Mose! I can't make trouble." Those words were so cowardly and so hard to say. But it was the truth. I could not make trouble for my family.

"You joking, right?" Mose said.

I shook my head. "If the Wilsons kicked us off their land, where would we go? Where would Mama find a job?"

Silence.

"Listen," I said. "First we have to find out *if* he took them. Then, if he did, we can decide what to do about it. We got to think, do this right."

"Yeah, well, he can't get me kicked out of my house," Mose spat.

Billy scowled, his arms crossed. "Now it makes sense."

"What does?"

"Something my brother said a couple days ago. I didn't think anything of it, except that Keet Wilson was getting weirder by the day."

"What did Jake say?"

"Couple things. First he said if Keet messed with us again he was going to go have a little face-to-face with him."

"Now you talking," Rico said.

"You told Jake?" I said. "He knows about the boat?"

"Jake's okay. He'll keep quiet about it."

I scowled. "Billy, you got to tell Jake not to mess with Keet, okay? No trouble. Just like I can't go to the police."

"Fine. I'll tell Jake we can handle it ourselves."

"What else did he say?"

Billy thought. "Well . . . this one is weird. Late in the afternoon, last Wednesday, Jake was cutting across the Wilsons' yard over to ours. He heard a truck coming up the driveway, so he turned to look. The truck passed by close enough for him to see Keet inside, not driving, but up front with two other guys. Jake knew the guys from school, and the driver waved at Jake."

"What's so weird about that?" I asked.

"Nothing, except that the truck was loaded up with something covered by a tarp. Jake wouldn't have thought anything about it, but then they did something strange."

"What you mean, strange?" Mose said.

"Instead of parking the truck in the driveway, they drove it right over the grass and into the trees, blazing a trail into the jungle."

21
DEEP
JUNGLE

"Ojii-chan," I said when I got home late that afternoon. "Go for a walk with me." He needed to walk, anyway. Mrs. Davis had stopped by to check up on him. "Remember to get him moving," she said, "but not too strenuously." I said, "He's moving around a lot," but I didn't tell her about Fumi.

Grampa Joji was sitting on the front steps deep in thought, keeping the dogs from bothering him with his foot.

Mama sat two steps above him. They weren't talking, just keeping each other company, I guess. Mama winked at me.

Ojii-chan scowled. He never went for a walk just to go for a walk. There had to be a reason, but he knew keeping the strokes away was the most important reason. He wasn't that dumb. Sometimes he got dizzy, and sometimes his vision got blurry, but other than that he was as good as he ever was. He was faking, was what I thought. And I was starting to think maybe Mrs. Davis knew it too—but was staying quiet about it to keep him out of that camp.

I glanced around for Little Bruiser. Nowhere in sight. "Come on, Grampa. This is important."

"Confonnit."

But he creaked up and stepped into his muddy rubber boots. I was barefoot, as always.

Mama stood and watched us walk off.

The deep jungle up behind the Wilsons' house was still wet from that morning's rain. Grampa's khaki pants grew dark to the knees. I knew by the way he'd stopped complaining that he was curious about where we were going. Hiking wasn't something we did together. But he wouldn't ask questions about what I was up to. He'd rather gag on American milk than give me an ounce of anything over him.

I made sure to stay clear of Keet's house, not wanting to stir up any curiosity. But once we were deep enough in the jungle, we cut back over that way, forging our own trail. When we hit the mashed-down grassy path the truck had made, we followed it deeper into the shadowy vine-bearded trees.

We hadn't gone far before we stumbled on what I was looking for.

Grampa scowled at the pile of boat parts. He squatted down to lay his fingers on the long shaft of the tiller, recognition growing on his face.

"From Papa's boat," I said.

It took a moment for Ojii-chan to form his question. "How come this stay here?" he finally said, breaking his unspoken rule of never asking me anything.

"Keet Wilson and some guys . . . they stole it from down by the boat and brought it up in a truck."

Grampa frowned deeper, still confused.

I squatted down next to him and told him what I was doing, step by step. "I know I can bring it up, Ojii-chan. I'm not sure how, but somehow I'm going to do it."

Grampa squinted, his eyes slits.

Said nothing.

"Grampa?"

For the first time in all of my life, Grampa Joji, looking straight into my eyes, into my brain, even—for the first time, he grinned at me.

His old stubby gray head bobbed.

"Unnh," he grunted. "Good, good . . . maybe you not so dumb as you look, nah?"

I had never received such a compliment from him in my life. A warm swelling in my chest rolled up into my throat.

Grampa tapped the tiller with a hand. "We take this, hide um."

"That's what I was thinking," I said. "Me and my friends are kind of worried, though." I lifted my chin back toward Keet's house. "He threatened to have me arrested. If we're not careful he could make big trouble for us, Ojii-chan."

"Unnh."

We were silent a moment, both of us thinking.

"Maybe I should just forget it," I whispered.

Grampa popped my knee with the back of his hand and glared at me.

"Ow!" I said. "What'd you do that for?"

"Kessite akirameruna!" he spat. "You can say that one time, but no more."

I studied him, rubbing my knee. "Okay, Ojii-chan. I won't give up."

"No worry."

Uh-oh. Now he had that rascal dancing in his eyes. "Don't worry? If we get caught, we could—"

Grampa Joji held up a hand. "You got *me* now, boy," he said. "I going help you."

22
SANJI'S TRUCK

Around noon the next day, Sunday, I sat in Billy's yard with his dog and the key to Sanji's truck, waiting for the Davises to get home from church.

I rubbed the key between my thumb and finger. *Was* this for Sanji's truck? Or was it was for something else? Maybe the pants weren't even Sanji's. But who cared about the pants? It was the truck I couldn't get out of my mind. In all this time, how could I not have thought about it?

"I'm losing it, Red," I mumbled, and Red thumped his tail on the grass. I stuck the key into my pocket and scratched his upturned belly.

Minutes later the Davises drove up and parked outside the garage. The black Ford Jake had been working on was still jacked up in there. Mr. and Mrs. Davis waved at me and headed into the house.

97

I lifted my chin, hello.

Jake went straight into the garage, still in his clean white church shirt. He squatted down to look at the underbelly of the black car.

Billy strolled over, undoing his tie. "What's up?" he said, stretching his neck to unbutton his collar. He folded his tie and stuck it in his back pocket.

I held up the key.

"Ahh," he said.

"Want to go take a look and see if it's still there?"

"Darn right. Hang on. I gotta change."

A half hour later we were sitting in the back of a half-empty Sunday bus heading for Kewalo Basin. I sat by the window, looking out at the people and cars and buildings that made Honolulu what it was, a busy mixture of everything you could think of—rich, not so rich, clean, dirty, nice, junky, loud, peaceful, generous. I loved this place. Even after it had been beaten up and scarred by war.

The bus headed down Queen Emma Street and passed the Pacific Club, just after a row of run-down shacks that some people had to call home. I gazed at the club as we drove by. Monkeypod trees spread out over a parking lot full of expensive cars in front of the low stucco building where Honolulu's rich went to eat, play tennis, swim, and do business.

"What you looking at?" Billy said.

"Nothing. Just remembering when Keet was a decent guy."

"You mean in his last life?"

"His dad belongs to that place," I said, nodding toward the club. "He took me there once."

"You're joking."

"No, really. It was before you moved here. We were just small kids then, and he invited me to go swimming. It's something else, that place, how rich people live." I shook my head, remembering how nice it was. "You can even get food by the pool."

"Did you know only men can be members?"

"Really?"

"True," Billy said. "That's how come my parents never joined. My mom won't step foot in that place until they change that rule."

"Huh."

We rode on in silence, me still thinking about how Keet and I had a good time swimming there. Funny to think how he was once an okay guy. What happened to him? That was the mystery. What changed him, really? Was it really just that I was Japanese, and only that? Somehow I didn't think so. There had to be more to it than that.

The harbor at Kewalo Basin was hot and quiet.

The sun, now heading out to sea, poured silver onto the light green water. Two old men sat out on the rocks at the mouth of the harbor with fishing poles, looking as sleepy as the boats lounging motionless at their moorings. One tuna boat leaned against the pier's black tire bumpers. The air smelled like dead fish. "Man, I miss going out on the boat with my dad," I said, breathing deep.

We headed over to the grove of coconut trees where Sanji had always parked.

And there it was.

It was covered with the dirt, dust, and grime of having sat

for too long in one spot. Its tires were pancaked out on the bottoms, but some air was left in them. The truck itself was kind of boxy looking, with wood sides around the bed, like a fence. Seeing it hit me like a slap in the face: one sunny day a year and a half ago Sanji had jumped out, thumped the door shut, and dropped that key into his pocket. That last day.

We stood staring at the abandoned truck.

Instantly, the memory of the stinky fish smell in the cab rushed back, the smell I hated but now would give anything to have back, just to sit in that cab with Sanji and Papa like in the before time.

"When Sanji parked it here he had no idea what was coming," Billy said.

"No."

I shook my head and looked across the harbor toward the pier. I didn't want to picture Sanji and Papa getting shot one more time.

"I wonder why nobody came and got it," Billy said.

"Good question."

"Got that key?"

I pulled it out and gave it to him. We went over and sat in the truck, Billy in the driver's seat. He stuck the key in the ignition and turned it. Nothing happened. "Dead as a rock," he said. "But this is the key, all right. Fits perfect."

We sat.

I started to sweat in the stuffy cab, flies buzzing in and out of the windows. I tried to open the glove box. It was rusted shut. Sanji was proud of his truck, and so lucky to have it. "You think we should go tell his wife about this?"

"Don't you think she already knows?"

"Well, maybe she doesn't know what to do with it."

"That could be."

"Let's stop by her place," I said. "It's only a little bit out of the way."

"She knows," Billy said.

"Yeah, but just to be sure."

"Fine."

We walked downtown, three or four miles away. Found the alley where Sanji's wife and daughter lived with Reiko's mother. Mama knew Reiko but hadn't visited in a long time. Maybe she should, I thought. Mama was stuck up in Nu'uanu with no Japanese friends to talk to.

The street was still as grimy as I remembered it, and clothes hung out of every window just like the last time me and Billy had gone there, right after Sanji was killed. We climbed the rickety wooden stairs.

"You knock," Billy said. "I'll stand behind you."

"Good idea."

Haoles made some people nervous, especially those who rarely talked to them, like Reiko and her mother. But they'd met Billy before.

I knocked and Mari opened the door, now a good two inches taller than the last time I'd seen her. She was about as tall as Kimi, up to my chest. Black hair cut short, and dimples in her cheeks.

She recognized Billy and brightened. Forget about me, she beamed straight in on Billy. On our one visit he'd given her the brand-new binoculars he'd just gotten for Christmas.

"Mama!" she shouted over her shoulder.

Reiko appeared behind her in shorts and an old shirt of

Sanji's that I recognized. Her hand flew to her hair, patting it down like Mama always did when somebody showed up unexpected. She was barefoot. "Oh, Tomikazu, how are you? And Billy, right? Long time no see, long time."

"Yeah, that's me," Billy said.

Reiko opened the door wider. "Come inside. Please."

The place was just as before, dark and crammed with odd pieces of furniture. I sat on one end of the couch. Reiko sat on the other. Mari stood next to Billy, who didn't know what to do, so he just stood with his hands clasped in front of him like you would at a funeral.

"How is your family?" Reiko asked.

"We're doing all right," I said. "My grampa came home."

Reiko cocked her head. "Came home? How can that be? I thought they arrested him."

"They did, but he's home now. He was at a camp on Kauai, and he had a stroke, so they brought him to Queen's Hospital. Billy's parents . . ."

I stopped, feeling the emotion rise in my chest.

Billy studied the floor.

"This is amazing," Reiko whispered.

"Yes."

Silence.

"There's more," I said. "I mean more that's amazing." I pulled the key out of my pocket and polished it with my thumb. Stared at it. Then handed it to her. "This is the key to Sanji's truck. I mean . . . well, I guess it's your truck now."

The key lay flat in Reiko's open palm. She looked up at me, her eyes beginning to swell with tears.

"I . . . the truck," she said, wiping tears with the back of her wrist. "I tried to sell it, but who can afford such a luxury these days? You can't even get the gas to put in it? I didn't know what to do with it, so . . ."

She fell silent, staring at the silver key in her hand.

Billy glanced at Mari, who smiled at him. He smiled back, then looked at his feet.

I rubbed my chin. "Maybe we can—"

I stopped to let the thought form.

Yeah, we could do it. "Listen, maybe me and Billy can fix it up and try to sell it for you," I said. "You could prob'ly use the money, right?"

Billy looked up.

"Maybe we could," I said.

Billy snapped his fingers. "Jake!" He looked at Reiko. "My brother could get it going again, absolutely. Then we could put an ad in the paper and—"

"What did you want for it when you tried to sell it?" I said, the idea now leaping in my mind.

"I don't know, fifty dollars? Whatever I could get."

Billy scrunched up his face, thinking. "Sounds low," he said. "But Jake would know."

We waited a moment longer; then I got up. "We need to get back home soon. So if it's okay with you, can we work on trying to sell it for you? Better than letting it rust and fall apart."

"You boys sell it," she said, grabbing my hand and pressing the key into my palm. "Keep the money. Sanji loved your father, Tomi. He would want you to have it."

We looked at each other, her eyes smiling with the memory of her good husband. She squeezed my hand shut, then let go.

"Thank you, really . . . but I think what he'd want was for you to have it. You and Mari."

Reiko pulled Mari to her side and hugged her. "Yes. Mari."

We left; Billy had already figured out the whole thing. "The hardest part will be getting Jake to fix it," he said. "He's pretty busy."

"Maybe we can pay him."

"Naw, it's never about money for him. But it should be if he's serious about saving up for a car. He'll do it if I have to drag him down there."

"Right. Like you even could?"

"I got ways."

"How?"

"Wait and see, bud. Like I said, I got ways."

"You so full of it."

Billy grinned and slapped my back.

23
THE WILSONS' HOUSE

Friday afternoon six days later, right after I got home from school, Mama came home early from the Wilsons'. She was wearing her white work apron and light blue dress, which Mrs. Wilson bought for her to wear when she cleaned their house. She smelled like bleach. "Come with me," she said. She grabbed my arm and pulled me toward the back door.

"Where's Kimi?" I asked. I was supposed to watch her after school.

"Charlie's place, planting seeds. Come."

"Where we going?"

"Wilson house."

I jerked my arm away. "No, Mama. I'm not going there."

She studied me. "I need you, Tomi-kun. I not strong enough."

"For what?"

"Move a big table and the rug underneath it. I need to clean the floor and you need to beat the rug outside."

"Get Keet to help you, or his dad."

Mama grabbed my arm again. "They gone Lanikai. Gone till Sunday. Come. I need you."

I let her pull me out the door. If she needed my help I would give it to her. But only because the Wilsons weren't home.

Keet's old dog, Rufus, came nosing up, then hobbled over to plop down in the shade. We went in the back door, like always.

In the kitchen Mama dropped her key into the pocket on her cleaning apron. Bright copper pots hung from a rectangular bar above the stove. The icebox was five times bigger than the one we had. A newspaper lay on the shiny red counter. "Mama, can we have this?" I said.

"That's where they leave it if I want it. Come with me."

I'd take the paper when we were done.

The wood floor felt smooth and solid under my bare feet, not like our floor, which was rough and often dusty. And also saggy, because our whole house was up off the ground. The Wilsons' house was sitting on concrete, with no space under it. I wondered why, because a house was raised up so the bugs and rats couldn't get in. But I didn't see any bugs or rats here.

"This the one," Mama said, showing me into the dining room. The long table was made of some dark wood, with ten chairs around it. That was strange, because only three people lived in that house, Keet and his parents. The rug under it was bigger than our whole kitchen.

"You want me to drag *this* rug out and beat it?"

"Use the broom. Hang it over the railing on the porch and hit it until no more dust. Then wipe the dust off the railing after you bring it back."

"You're serious?"

"Lift up that end. We move the table over by the window."

I rolled up the rug and dragged it out to the porch, sweating. Mama filled a metal bucket with soapy water and got down on her hands and knees to wipe the wood floor spotless.

It was easier to bring a fifty-pound tuna up from the bottom of the sea than it was to get that rug up over the railing. Sweat poured into my eyes, the heat sucking water out of me like a bilge pump. I went back into the house to find a broom.

I looked at the long, sleek wood railing and dark wood stairs leading up to the second floor.

And the doors above them.

Keet's door.

I shouldn't.

I could hear Mama rubbing out the dirt that probably wasn't even there. I looked back up the stairs. She'd never know.

The steps were solid. A carpet ran up the middle. Soundless.

I knew which room was Keet's, because a long time ago I came over to his house a few times. I never got farther than the front room, but I saw him run up to his bedroom to get things we could play with. His mother never let me go upstairs.

His was the second door. Closed.

The white porcelain doorknob turned without squeaking. I peeked back over the railing, listening for Mama. I probably had three minutes before she started wondering where I was. She knew I didn't have that broom.

I eased open Keet's door.

A path of sunlight fell through the window onto twisted sheets crunched down at the foot of the bed. The closet door gaped open. What surprised me the most was what I didn't see—things. Like in Billy's room, where he had models and baseball stuff and pictures on the wall. Keet's room was almost empty. A triangular pennant was tacked to the wall above his bed that read NAVY—yellow letters on a dark blue background.

I crept over to his dresser—a ship in a bottle and two small metal airplanes on top, two drawers half open with clothes bulging out. Above, a mirror glared back at me, one I couldn't look into, the guilt of being there heavy on my shoulders. A photograph stood just behind the bottled ship. It was of Keet around ten years old, standing between two men. One was his father and the other a navy guy, looked like an officer. Behind them was a battleship at berth. Keet was smiling at the camera. Happy.

I peeked in his closet and found two rifles, one a BB gun, the other a .22, the one he'd shot our family katana with in the jungle. Remembering that made my eyes squint down. There was something else in that closet too, coiled up and hanging on a peg. A woven leather bullwhip. I touched it, took it off the peg, felt its weight, smelled its sweet new-leather smell.

I put it back.

I wiped my sweaty hands on my pants. Even though Mama had said the Wilsons were away for the weekend, my mind screamed: *Get out! You shouldn't be here.* I headed toward the door.

Then froze.

There was something under Keet's bed.

My heart seemed to stop.

Burlap!

I knew what it was the second I saw it.

I crept over, squatted down, and pulled it out.

Unfolded the *furoshiki* scarf inside the burlap.

Tiny needles prickled all over my scalp, because there on the floor shining in the sunlight was our family katana, the samurai sword that I had hidden in the jungle.

Keet had found it!

I stood, quickly wrapping it back up, my jaw tight with a rage I'd never felt before, ever. Even Papa would feel that same anger.

Mama had to know.

She was still on her knees scrubbing the floor.

I ran down the stairs and stood in the dining room doorway. She felt me behind her and stopped scrubbing to look back. "What, Tomi-kun?"

I held up the burlap and unwrapped the katana. "I found this in Keet's room, under his bed."

Mama pushed herself to her feet, dropping the rag into the bucket of water. "You were in his room?"

"I just wanted to see it."

She came over and held her hand over the blade but didn't touch it.

"I hid it in the jungle, Mama, and he found it and took it." I paused, thinking. "I'm taking it home."

"No."

I gaped at her. "No?"

"We will be accused of stealing, Tomi-kun. You must leave it."

"Stealing? Mama, it's ours!"

"We need this work, we need our home. If we are accused of stealing we will lose all of it."

"But *he* stole it, not me."

"He found it."

I stared at her, clutching the katana to my chest. I had promised Grampa I would take care of it. Nothing we had was as important as the family katana, the symbol of generations of family strength, and honor.

"Mama—"

"Put it back. We will find another way."

We stared at each other. Lines I hadn't noticed before trailed across her forehead. But the look in her eyes told me the real story. Mama wasn't getting older; she was getting stronger.

And she was right.

I mashed my lips together. Never in all my life was anything so hard as climbing the stairs back to Keet Wilson's bedroom.

24
BRILLIANT
RICO

A week later Grampa Joji made me take him down to the boat. It was Saturday, and we could work all day. The katana was still on my mind, but I'd settled with it. I would get it back somehow, sometime. No question.

Billy went over to get Mose and Rico, and they met me and Grampa Joji at the canal. But none of them were sure of how to act with grumpy Grampa around. They glanced sideways at him and stood around saying nothing.

"He won't bite you," I whispered.

Mose and Rico put on goggles and grabbed a couple of wrenches, anxious to get in the water. There were a few more things we could remove from the boat. After today we would have only the impossible left.

Grampa squatted on his heels at the edge of the canal.

"Go," he said to me, nodding toward the boat. "I going think."

I frowned: You think you can come up with something we didn't?

Billy and I grabbed goggles and jumped off the rocks.

Grampa picked up a large rock and lifted it, like lifting weights in a gym. Exercising while he thought, the way Mrs. Davis had showed him.

When Grampa and I had found the boat parts in the jungle behind Keet's house, we decided to leave them exactly where they were. They would be safer there than anywhere else, because Keet wouldn't steal from his own hiding place. Later, when we were ready, I'd get as many guys as I could and go up there and get them.

But right now I had two huge problems.

One—get the boat up and float it down the canal and over to Kewalo Basin, where we could get it onto land, dry it out, and repair it.

And two—deal with Keet Wilson, and anyone else who believed we were bringing the *Taiyo Maru* up to get it back into action on the side of the enemy.

Grumpy or not, I was glad Grampa Joji had come along. He made me feel stronger, just by believing in what we were doing. With him and all my friends I was feeling pretty good.

"Hey," I said to Billy after we'd both come up for air. "You ask Jake about fixing up that truck yet?"

"Done deal."

"He'll do it?"

"Piece of cake."

I raised my eyebrows. "What'd you have to do for him?" There was always a catch.

Billy wiped the water from his face and shrugged.

"Come on, tell me."

"Okay, fine, I said I'd take over his job of taking out the garbage."

"For how long?"

"We got work to do, let's go back down."

"Come on," I said. "How long?"

"A year."

"What! That's the best you could do? Some negotiator."

Billy laughed. "Small price to pay, son."

I smiled. "Yeah, you right."

I looked back toward shore. "Where's Grampa?"

"Huh," Billy said. "Maybe he got bored."

Mose and Rico popped up. "What's going on?" Rico said. "You two not working today or what?"

"Grampa Joji's gone."

We climbed up out of the water. Billy stood dripping, hands on his hips. The small pile of things from inside the boat lay strewn at his feet—two coils of rope, some canned food, three empty buckets, and two soggy blankets. "Looks like we've finished the easy part."

"Now what?" I mumbled.

We stood brooding. I looked around for Grampa, but he was nowhere in sight. Boy, sometimes he drove me crazy.

Rico snapped his fingers. "I know what we need now—muscle. How's about we try go get that Kaka'ako Frankenstein, the guy Gayle the Whale, the Butcher? Remember him? He could help us pull up this boat."

"We could get all those guys," Mose added. His face lit up. "Yeah! They would help us, I know they would."

Billy snickered, shaking his head. "Won't work. Even with all those guys, and even more guys, if you could convince them to break their backs for us—the boat is completely full of water, and water is about the heaviest thing you can imagine. It would take about five hundred guys as big as the Butcher to drag this boat up."

"Hey, ain't no time to go sissy, haole boy," Rico said. "You got to believe, ah? You want it, go get it. That's what Uncle Ramos always saying . . . right?"

"Wait," I said, a thought beginning to form. "Both of you are right. It would take five hundred guys, and thinking of the Kaka'ako guys was brilliant, Rico, because you know what? You remember the second-base guy, Herbie Okubo? Guess what his pops is . . . a boatbuilder."

Rico puffed up his chest when he heard that he was brilliant. He flicked his eyebrows at Mose, who said, "One good thought that you don't even know you had don't make you brilliant, brah."

"Herbie's pop *repairs* boats too," I said. "My dad had him work on ours a couple times, and he can probably help us drag it out of the water, too. All we have to do is get it up and float it down to Kewalo."

"Good plan," Billy said. "But . . ."

Another thought was coming. "Yeah," I whispered, "yeah, yeah, yeah!"

"What you thinking, brah?" Mose said.

"We don't have to bring this boat up *all* the way," I said.

"We only have to get it off the mud . . . just enough to drag it away."

"Okay, fine," Billy said. "But how?"

"I don't know yet."

"Ask Rico," Mose said. "He look stupit, but he's brilliant, right, Rico?"

Rico grinned. "That's me."

Jeese.

25
CRAZY OLD COOT

When I got home later that afternoon, the lowering sun was stabbing long tree shadows across the face of our small green house. Like always, Lucky came out to greet me. Little Bruiser was over in the weeds, his knobby head cocked my way.

Mama sat on the steps watching me come up the path.

"What are you doing?" I asked. It was strange to see her sitting there alone, doing nothing. It wasn't like her.

"Look at this yard," she said.

I glanced around. "What about it?"

"It looks sad."

"Sad?"

Mama didn't go on. She tried to smile, but it only made her look lonely. It was hard for her, living up here with no other Japanese families around. "Where is Ojii-chan?" she said.

116

"He's not here?"

Little Bruiser took a few steps toward me, then stopped. I kept him in the corner of my eye as I knelt down to pet Lucky.

"He went with you," Mama said. "Where is he?"

That old man was complicating my life. "He disappeared on me about three hours ago. I thought he got tired and came home."

"He's not here, you need to find him. He comes, he goes, he disappears from right beside you, then he show up like a ghost." Mama put her hands on her knees and pushed herself up. "Just find him, Tomi-kun."

I sighed. "You know what I think, Mama? I think he keeps moving around because he's so happy to be out of that prison camp."

She tilted her head and studied me. "Maybe." She looked up at the sky, now blue gray as night rolled down. "Big trouble if he gets caught after curfew."

"I know, Mama, but where should I look?"

She turned to go back in the house. "Just find him."

"Crazy old coot," I mumbled. "Yeah, you too," I added, glancing over at Little Bruiser, now one or two steps closer. "Come on, Lucky, let's go see what we can see, huh?"

Mama was right to be worried. If Grampa was out at night anything could happen to him. He could get lost, shot, or arrested. Again.

I jogged back toward the street with Lucky loping out ahead.

We didn't have to go very far, because Ojii-chan was right at the end of the path—with a BMTC guy's rifle pointed at his chest.

"Don't get smart with me, old man," the BMTC guy said. "Because I'm the one with the gun and you're the one who should be off the streets."

Grampa glared at the BMTC, who was maybe thirty years old. Ojii-chan took a step forward. The guy took a step back, raising the rifle to Grampa's face. "Halt!"

"Wait!" I shouted, running up. "He's my grandfather. I'll take him home."

The BMTC's eyes darted between mine and Grampa's.

I grabbed Grampa's arm and tugged. "Come home, Ojii-chan. It's curfew."

Grampa wouldn't budge, his eyes slicing up the BMTC guy.

"I could take him in, kid. Quick as spit."

"Yessir, you sure could, but he lives here, right up this path. He's almost home. He was just a little late."

"Yeah, well—"

"Come on, Ojii-chan. Let's go home."

Grampa finally eased off and turned to head home. "Confonnit," he mumbled.

I nodded to the BMTC guy and followed Grampa Joji up the path.

"Where *were* you, Ojii-chan?" I whispered.

Grampa winked. "You see that mans's eye? He scared of me."

"Jeese, Grampa, you can't go around challenging them, you know. They're not fooling. They could shoot you and no one would even make a peep about it. We the enemy to them, you and me. And not only that, you could get the Davises in

118

trouble, because they're responsible for you. Remember? They got you released? You got to be good."

"Bah," he spat, waving me off.

"Anyway, I thought you came home before me," I said.

Of course he ignored me, just kept on heading up to the house. "Watch out the goat," he said, then cackled.

Jeese. Something about him was different. What?

Something was off. I scowled and followed him toward the steps, Little Bruiser trotting toward me.

Mama came out and held the screen door open. Grampa brushed by and went into the house. She gave me a look that said: *You should have stayed with him.*

"What?" I said, turning my palms out.

"Come inside. Eat."

I started up the wooden steps.

"You lucky Ojii-chan didn't get mad that you left him."

"Left him? He left *me.*"

"Come inside."

Lucky he didn't get—

Hey! *That's* what was off about him. He wasn't scowling. He wasn't grumpy. And what was with that winking? Was he . . . happy?

Naah, couldn't be.

What did that old cockaroach have up his sleeve?

26
OKUBO'S BOATYARD

The next day, Sunday, me and Billy took the bus over to Mose and Rico's neighborhood; then the four of us braved up and headed down into enemy territory—Kaka'ako.

The only guys who welcomed us there were the baseball guys we used to play against before the war, the Kaka'ako Boys. Everyone else eyed us with suspicion. The worst part about going down into that area on the Waikiki side of downtown Honolulu was a gang of punks we called the Centipede Boys. They didn't like strangers coming into their territory, and they especially didn't like haoles like Billy, who stuck out like the moon on a black night.

We got lucky. No Centipede Boys in sight.

"Remember when coming here used to be the spookiest thing we did?" Billy said. "Now, with this war, it's nothing."

"Spooky?" Rico said. "You was scared? Those punks don't worry me."

"Talk big, ah, you?" Mose said. "You face down the Butcher, you going wet your pants."

"Pfff."

Mose chuckled. "You ain't been the same since you got shot in your face."

Rico shoved Mose, and Mose staggered off, laughing like the rest of us.

"Hanabatas . . . all of you," Rico said.

Okubo's Boatyard was down by the ocean, near Kewalo Basin, where Papa's boat used to harbor. And where Sanji's truck still sat, rusting. I reached into my pocket and rubbed the key, which I carried around like a good-luck charm. I needed some luck. I hoped I'd find some at the boatyard.

I'd met Mr. Okubo a couple of times with Papa when we went to him with boat problems. He was stiff in the old way, like Grampa. He was also the father of one of the Kaka'ako Boys—Herbie, at second base, a good guy.

I hoped Herbie would be around the boatyard, because I didn't know where his house was, and we sure didn't want to be drifting around Kaka'ako looking for it.

The boatyard was a big shed on the water, with an open yard to the side, where two sampans sat in dry-dock cradles, in for repair or repainting. Inside the shed was where Mr. Okubo built the new ones.

A scraggly dog eyed us from the entrance.

"Man, that dog is ugly," Rico said, wincing. "Looks like it got kicked around and ain't too happy about it."

He squatted down and stuck out his hand, making kissy sounds. "Here doggy, doggy, I not going kick you."

The dog growled, scarily deep for such a small dog. Rico jumped up.

"He says you ugly too," Mose said.

"What you going say to Mr. Okubo, Tomi?" Rico said.

"I have no idea."

"Well, I hope he's more nice than his dog."

"Ask him where Herbie is," Billy said. "Then we can ask Herbie to ask his dad if he has any ideas that could help us."

"Good idea. Let's go inside." We squeaked past the growling dog, who crouched, ready to fly at us if we made a wrong move. That mutt would have a dog like mine for lunch.

We got lucky. Herbie was there. His jaw dropped when we slouched in.

"Heyyy," I said. "Howzit?"

"Holy moly," he said. "You folks lost or something?"

"Naah," Rico said. "We came to see your dog."

Herbie laughed. "You met Sharky, huh? My brother Eddy's dog. He's in the army."

"Who?" Rico said. "The dog?"

"Shuddup, you fool," Mose said.

"I remember your brother," I said. "He came to see us play that one time, right?"

"He was home on leave."

"Yeah-yeah."

"He's somewhere in Europe now."

I nodded, then shook my head. Poor guy. I'd been reading

about our war with the Germans in the paper. Spooky, what was going on—all over the world.

We stood wondering what to do next. This was enemy territory, even if we did know Herbie.

"Uh . . . you . . . you got a minute to talk about something?" I said.

Herbie picked up a rag and wiped his hands. "Sure. I was just cleaning up. Let's go out back. Pop and Bunichi—that's a guy who works for him—they down at Pearl Harbor."

"Doing what?" Billy said.

"Fixing boats. What a mess they got down there . . . even now. Come," Herbie said.

We followed him around a brand-new sampan his dad was finishing up. *Red Hibiscus* was painted across the back of it. "Nice boat," I said.

Herbie nodded. "Second time Pop built this one. The first one burned."

"Ho, really?"

"The day it was finished we anchored it in the harbor for the night. Next morning it was underwater."

"Why?" I said.

Herbie shrugged. "Nobody knows. Just burned up. I saw it go down."

"Bad luck," Mose said.

"Took Pop forever to make this new one, with Eddy gone and all that work in Pearl Harbor."

Herbie led us out back into the sun. The ocean was right there, light blue and flat as a pond, with two tiny boat specks crawling along the horizon.

"Wow," I said. "Nice."

We sat on the rocks at the edge of the sea.

"What's up?" Herbie said.

"A sunken boat."

"I guess I should have said what's down, then." He grinned.

"Way down. My father's boat sank in the Ala Wai Canal with a bunch of boats."

Herbie bobbed his head. "I heard about those. Ten of them, right? Sampans?"

"That's them."

"And your pop's is one of them?"

"We've been trying to bring it back up," I said.

"We? Who's we?"

"Us," I said motioning to Billy, Mose, and Rico.

"Just you?"

I nodded.

Herbie gazed at me a moment. "Huh . . . you four guys and what? A crane?"

"No. Only us."

"But how can you bring up a sunken boat without a crane?"

"I don't know yet," I said, "but if we do, can we bring it here for your father to fix?"

"Well, sure, of course."

We sat watching the ocean.

"If you can get it here," Herbie said, "then Pop could get some guys and . . ." He glanced at me again. "Man . . . you need a crane."

Rico tossed a stone into the ocean.

Mose leaned back on his hands, closed his eyes, and raised his face to the sun.

"Well," I said. "At least I know I got somewhere to bring it if I can float it."

"Pop would fix it for free, I know he would."

"Really? I was thinking maybe I could work it off."

I gazed down the coast, trying to hide my discouragement, because even Herbie thought it was impossible, and he should know.

"I'm telling you," Herbie said. "You need a crane."

After a moment, I looked sideways at him and winked. "Or a good idea."

"Pfff."

27
THE
TENNIS
BALL

A couple of weeks later that good idea hit me like a slap in the face. It was the first week in May. I'd just gotten home from school.

Kimi had the job of washing clothes. She did that out back in a steel washtub filled with water warmed on our kerosene stove. She was out there scrubbing away on the washboard when Mama asked me to go out and check on her. It was a big job for a seven-year-old. But Kimi only wanted my help if she absolutely couldn't do something by herself.

Her dog, Azuki Bean, was lounging in the shade nearby, chewing on somebody's tennis ball. I squatted down and pulled the gooey thing from her mouth. "Where'd you get this? The Wilsons' court?"

I looked up and glanced around. For once that dumb goat was nowhere in sight. "Where's Grampa?"

"With the chickens," Kimi said, still scrubbing. She looked happy.

I stood and bounced the tennis ball off the hard dirt.

"Where did you get that?" Kimi said.

"Your dog got it somewhere."

Kimi stopped scrubbing and dried her hands on her shirt. "Can I see it?"

"Sure."

I bounced it to her. It went over her head and landed in the washtub. Kimi pushed it under, then let it pop back up. She did it again, giggling and trying to make it pop up higher.

It must be nice to have no problems, I thought. "Hey," I said. "I gotta go."

"Bye," she said, handing me the ball.

"Keep it."

Kimi smiled and dropped it back in the water.

Grampa had nineteen egg-laying chickens that he kept in five wooden chicken coops up in the bushes, just out of view behind the house.

I found him with his bucket, poking around for eggs. So far he had eight. Grampa handed me the bucket. "Take," he said, jerking his head toward the Wilsons' house. Because we lived on their land, and they employed Mama, we gave them eggs whenever we had them.

I shook my head. "I told you before, Ojii-chan. I'm done taking eggs over to that house. You do it."

Grampa scowled at me. We'd been through this, and he knew I was serious. But even though he knew Keet stole our boat parts, and even though it was the Wilsons who probably got him arrested after Pearl Harbor got bombed—even after all that, Grampa *still* felt an obligation to include the Wilsons in whatever we produced on their property—chickens for meat, eggs, tomatoes, lettuce, and string beans from what Charlie brought over to us, and even fish, whenever we got some.

"Confonnit," Grampa mumbled, and headed up to the Wilsons' himself.

"Watch out for Rufus," I called. "He don't like grumpy old men!"

My mind suddenly locked back on the washtub.

The *tennis ball!*

I pounded back down the muddy path to Kimi, tripping and stumbling like a drunken sailor, because now I knew how I was going to raise that boat.

28
FLASH-BANG
IDEA

The next morning, just after we got dropped off at school, I told Billy about my flash-bang idea. It wasn't something I wanted to talk about in front of Mr. and Mrs. Davis, because maybe us being down by the boat wasn't something we were supposed to be doing. I still needed to look into that. The last thing I wanted was to be on the wrong side of the military.

"Hmmm," Billy said, thinking. "Inner tubes."

"From old car tires."

The tennis ball had given me the idea of using trapped air to lift the boat off the bottom of the canal—holding the ball underwater, letting it pop back up. Bingo, I thought—inner tubes from old car tires! How many would it take?

"I don't think it will work," Billy said. "You'd need too

many of them. And now you can't get them because the army needs the rubber."

"Yeah, but maybe we can find some."

He shook his head. "Where?"

"How about your dad? He could get some."

"Some, maybe, but not enough."

Billy frowned, thinking as we headed up the grassy slope toward another day of school, where I could hardly sit still. I needed to be working down at the *Taiyo Maru,* not wasting my days at a beat-up desk thinking about it.

I knew I was wrong to think that I didn't need to be at school; it was good; it was important. Still, that boat was sitting underwater getting ruined, and I was running out of time. Summer was only a few weeks away, but I'd have less time then, because I'd have to get a job. I winced. I had to start asking around, starting at the cannery.

We sat on the grass outside the school, waiting for Mose and Rico. Soon they came strolling across the busy street, making cars slow down for them as if they owned the place.

They plopped down next to us. "Too nice for go inside today," Rico said.

"Just what I was thinking," I said.

Billy nudged Mose with his elbow. "You got to hear Tomi's bright idea."

"Yeah?"

I clapped my hands together. "Okay, listen." I told them about the inner tubes. "All I need is enough clearance to float the hull down the canal to Kewalo Basin, like Herbie said."

Rico thought it was a great idea. "But what I don't get," he added, "is how you going inflate all those tubes underwater? You can't push those things down like a tennis ball, you know."

"I have an idea for that."

But I didn't. Not yet.

"Okay," Mose said. "Say you could do that. Say the tubes could lift up the hull. Fine. But you still got a problem way more worse than that—the army, ah? They need rubber, right? Everybody collecting it now. No way they going let you use it when they need it so badly. And what about this— you ever wondered if the army going let you bring up that boat at all? They put those boats there for a reason. You might be out of luck, brah."

"Yeah," Rico said, "but that was before, when the war was on top of us. What about now? Maybe they forgot about them."

I shrugged. "Who knows?"

But if the army had forgotten about those boats . . .

"Anyway, say the army didn't care, and say we managed to collect fifty or sixty inner tubes," Billy said. "And we brought them all down to the boat—then we got caught. We could say we were just collecting them for the army, which wouldn't be a lie because right after we use them to float the boat, we could give them to a collection center."

"Ho!" Rico said. "With that much rubber we'd be heroes!"

"Yeah."

"Yeah."

But then we fell silent.

Because I don't think one of us believed we could ever collect enough tubes to make the boat go up even one half inch.

29
THE RED FISH

Four colorful fish streamers swam in the breeze on a bamboo pole above my house when I got home. *Koi-nobori.* Carp made of paper, looking like kites, but hollow inside. The air went in the mouth and blew them up fat.

"Wow," Billy said. "It's already Boys' Day again?"

"Yeah. Today is May fifth."

"I thought you hid all your Japanese stuff."

"Me too." Mama was taking a chance—for me. She shouldn't have put them up. They could get us in trouble. Probably not with the military, but for sure with Mr. Wilson.

The fish looked almost liquid, the way they waggled, so smooth and easy. "You think I should take them down?"

"Why?"

"Well . . . it's a Japanese thing, and you know Mr. Wilson."

Billy grinned. "Leave it up. Nobody can see this place from the road."

I shrugged. "Yeah. One or two days won't hurt. Besides, he hardly ever comes over here."

But still . . .

Mama or Grampa had planted the bamboo pole near the side of the house so that the fish could fly above the roof. To most haoles it was probably a strange tradition. But Billy didn't think so, and it made me feel good every year when Japanese celebrated all the boys in the house. If there were three boys, say, then there would be one fish for each of them—first, the two at the top were for the mom and pop, then the boys below—red, blue, and white koi.

The koi was a symbol of masculinity and strength because it was a fish that could swim upstream against strong currents. It persevered and lived a long life. Old-time stories even said koi used to swim all the way to heaven to become dragons.

Tango-no-Sekku, it was called—Boys' Day.

Just below Papa's and Mama's blue and white ones was me—the red fish, a dragon in the making.

"Later," Billy said, hurrying over to his house before Little Bruiser came bouncing out with his head down. "By the way," he said, stopping to look back. "Jake said we can go take a look at that truck this week or next, sometime after school."

"Great!"

"Keep that key handy."

I tapped my pocket. "I carry it everywhere." I started up

the steps and stopped. "Hey," I called. "Ask your dad about the inner tubes."

"Don't get your hopes up. It's hard to get hold of just about everything these days."

"Yeah, but ask anyway, all right?"

Billy turned and waved over his head without looking back.

Only Mama was home, the house silent. She was sitting at the kitchen table drinking tea after a long day at the Wilsons'.

"Mama, you shouldn't have put up those fish."

"Why?"

"Well . . . Mr. Wilson, he—"

She waved my words away. "Sometimes you have to do what you have to do."

"Mama?"

"This is your day, Tomi-kun."

I nodded. She could be stubborn when she wanted to.

"Where's Grampa?" I said.

"He took Kimi down to see his friend."

"You mean Fumi?"

Mama rolled her eyes and smiled. "Ojii-chan is Ojii-chan."

"You got that right." I sat down across from her and slapped my schoolbooks on the table. "Homework."

She reached across and patted my hand. "You good boy, Tomi-kun. Work hard."

I smiled but felt guilty because I wasn't working all that hard on what she thought I was.

Mama rinsed her cup and headed into the front room to clean up our house after spending the day cleaning the Wilsons'. But she stopped and looked back. I thought she would smile or say something. But she turned and left the kitchen, keeping her thought to herself.

I sat gazing out the window, thinking of Mama and Mrs. Wilson. How uneven this world was. Some people worked and struggled. Some people didn't.

Little Bruiser came into view in the bushes outside the window. His head was perked, looking at something in the trees that I couldn't see.

I sighed and opened my math book, my hardest subject, especially long, confusing word problems that tangled up my brain. Sometimes I'd almost rather take eggs up to the Wilsons' house than do them.

A few minutes later I was lost, trying to work one of them out, when something in the trees moved in the corner of my eye. I looked up, waiting for it to move again.

There!

Little Bruiser streaked into the trees. I heard a muffled yelp.

Keet Wilson! He was slinking around our house, using the trees for cover.

I put my pencil down.

"Mama?" I called.

She didn't answer.

"Mama, you in the house?"

Still no answer.

I got up and went into the front room. I saw her outside

through the screen door, standing in the yard with her back to the house.

I eased open the squeaky door. "Mama?"

She turned to look back over her shoulder and in her hands I could see the fish kites torn to shreds. She held the pieces up.

"Tst," I spat, and jumped down off the porch without using the steps. The screen door slapped shut behind me.

The bamboo pole the fish had been tied to had been ripped out and broken, two sad pieces at her feet. "Keet did this?"

Mama nodded. "I was standing right here."

"He did it in *front* of you?"

Mama was silent for a moment, as if wanting to say more, and wanting not to as well. "When . . . when he tore them up, he looked at me, right in my eye. I was too shocked to speak."

"Did he say anything?"

Mama nodded but offered nothing.

"What, Mama? What did he say?"

She wouldn't look at me.

"He said, 'No Japanese symbols on our land—understand? Next time I going call police.' "

"What!"

"He's angry boy, Tomi-kun. You stay away from him."

"I want to, Mama, believe me . . . but I don't think that's going to be possible."

"What you mean?"

I looked off into the trees, over toward the Wilsons'

house, big, white glimpses of it peeking through the branches.

"Mama . . . he's not getting away with this, no." I took the torn-up *koi-nobori* from her.

"Tomi—"

"Don't worry, Mama. I'm not going to do anything stupid."

I took the torn fish streamers into the house and put the pieces under my mattress. I would tape them back together and get a new bamboo pole, because for sure, when Papa came home after the war, those fish would fly again.

Especially the red one.

Over this house.

On the Wilsons' property.

And Keet Wilson would have to go through me if he wanted to tear them up again.

30
MR. UNCLE RAMOS

On Friday at school just after lunch, me, Billy, Mose, and Rico were sitting in our usual sunny place, leaning up against the side of the building. Mr. Ramos wandered by and waved. We waved back, and he walked on.

Then he stopped and came back.

He eased down and sat in the dirt between me and Rico.

We sat silent. He'd never done this before, and who ever saw a teacher sitting in the dirt with students?

Mr. Ramos put his knees up and rested his arms on them. "So," he said, then waited a moment, thinking.

Rico glanced at him. We all did.

"I heard your grandfather came home, Tomi."

"Yeah," I whispered, turning away. I didn't want to spread that around, thinking if too many people heard about it, the army might think we were bragging and take Grampa away again.

He chuckled. "Good news gets around."

"Billy's parents did it. They got him released because . . . he had a stroke, and—"

"And he shouldn't have been arrested in the first place," Mr. Ramos said.

I nodded. "So Billy's parents took responsibility for him."

Mr. Ramos reached over and tapped Billy's knee.

"You know how rare it is that he got released?" he said, turning back to me.

I looked at him.

"He's the only one I've heard of," he said.

I shook my head, considering our good fortune.

"We're lucky here in the islands," Mr. Ramos went on. "On the mainland they took all the Japanese from the coast and put them in camps, everyone. Here they didn't do that. You boys know why?"

We shook our heads.

"Labor," he said. "If they put all our Japanese in camps our economy would fall apart."

I nodded, wondering if I knew what that meant.

"I heard something else, too," Mr. Ramos said. "About a boat."

"Uh . . ."

Mr. Ramos chuckled. "You didn't know I knew that, right?"

Stupid Rico. It was him that told, like always.

"Don't worry," Mr. Ramos said. "I'm not going to try to stop you and I'm not going to spread that knowledge around, either. I know what you're thinking, because I was your age once too, believe it or not. Right now you're thinking about how you're going to get whoever told me that, right? And you're thinking it was Rico or Mosc, right?"

I nodded again.

He shook his head, smiling.

I glared past Mr. Ramos at Rico.

Rico shrugged and looked away.

"Listen, Tomi," Mr. Ramos went on. "It was Rico who told me, but don't blame him. He came to me because he is your good friend and he was worried about you."

"Worried?"

Mr. Ramos turned to Rico. "Tell him."

"Well," Rico said. "The way I been thinking, if the army catch you fooling around that boat . . . that they put up in the canal for some reason . . . they might think you're a traitor for messing with it, and arrest you . . . and maybe even your grampa . . . put you both in jail, you know?"

I frowned. Stared at a scabby scratch on the back of my thumb. I'd had that same thought myself, but I'd been shoving it out of my head every time it came to me.

I nodded. "Yeah."

"So I looked into it," Mr. Ramos said. "I made some calls, trying to find out what the military had in mind for those sampans. And guess what?"

"They're going to toss me in jail?"

"Hah! No. They didn't even remember those boats. So I asked about salvaging one of them, and the guy said he didn't think the army would care, so long as the boats were never used . . . at least, while the war is on."

"So I won't get in trouble?"

"Not from them. But if you do, you call me, all right?"

"Yeah, yeah, I will. Thanks, Mr. Ramos."

"Thank Rico."

"Yeah, Rico, thanks."

"No problem."

Mr. Ramos pushed himself up with a grunt and brushed off the back of his pants. "That's about the most uncomfortable place to sit that I can think of."

We all grinned.

Mr. Ramos walked away, whistling.

"You punks got the best uncle," I said. "The best."

"Hey!" Mose called to Mr. Uncle Ramos. "You still got dirt on your pants."

Without turning back, Mr. Ramos slapped a hand over his rear end and flashed us a low-handed shaka sign: Thanks.

31
THE
WRECK

After school, Jake drove me and Billy down to Kewalo Basin in the black Ford he was fixing up. "A test drive," he said. "See how she runs."

"You some kind of a mechanic now?" Billy said.

Jake snorted. "You a dead little brother now?"

Billy laughed. I shook my head and watched the world go by, so much faster in that car than on a city bus. Someday I hoped I would have a car. It would be black, of course . . . and polished up so glassy you could comb your hair in the reflection.

We drove slowly when we got to the harbor, inching past the pier over toward the vacant land beyond. Jake parked in the trees near the hulk of Sanji's truck. A huge palm frond had fallen on it, brown and crinkly.

"This is what you want to get going again?" Jake said.

"That's it."

We parked and got out. Billy dragged the dried-up frond off the hood, then opened up the driver's-side door and slapped his hand on the seat. A cloud of dust poofed up. Billy coughed and stepped back. "That's what you get for leaving the windows down."

"You got the key to this thing?" Jake said.

I dug it out and gave it to him.

Jake slipped in behind the wheel, not caring if the seat was dirty. He tried the ignition, just like we had. "You got to try the obvious first," he said, grinning.

He got out and went around to open up the hood. He propped it up and stuck his head in, poking around every grimy part in that engine. "If the fuel line is clear, and the pump works . . . get a new battery . . . we can probably get this thing going. Then I can drive it home and clean up the engine, and you kids could wash it and clean up the wheels and tires, and then we can sell it. I think we could get maybe a hundred dollars or we could ask for a hundred and twenty-five, then come down to a hundred. Something like that."

"Need to get some air in those tires," I said.

Jake squatted down to check each of them. "Just enough left in them to hobble over to the nearest service station." He stood. "Boy," he said to me. "Grab my tool box."

"Yessir," I said, grinning.

Jake was black with grime to his elbows by the time he'd gotten the battery out. He handed it to me. "Put this in the trunk of the Ford."

I sagged under its weight.

"We got to get that recharged," Jake said. "Or buy a new one."

Back over at the pier, we washed our hands from a spigot. A man from the fish shed headed toward us. "Saw you boys over there in the trees. You going get that wreck out of here?"

"Yessir," Jake said.

"Good," the guy said. "Does it run?"

"Well, not yet."

"I hate to see a good truck waste away like that."

We all looked across the harbor toward the truck. "Too bad about Sanji," the man said.

"You knew him?" I said.

"Of course. Good man. I know you, too," he said to me. "Taro's boy, right?"

"You know my dad?"

"I'm Jimmy Hiroki," he said, sticking out his hand to shake. "I work in the shed. I know every fisherman in Honolulu." He shook his head. "Too bad your daddy got arrested."

I looked down.

"How come nobody came for that truck before?" he said.

"Sanji's wife didn't know what to do with it, so we're going to try to fix it up and sell it for her."

"Yeah, good." He shook his head. "Bad for everybody, this war."

"Yeah," we muttered.

"Hey," the guy added. "Push it over behind the shed. I got an air pump. You can fill the tires, at least. I seen how flat they are."

Jake's face lit up. "That'd help a ton. Thanks."

The man waved him off. "Least I could do."

"Got to do something, you know?" I said. "For Sanji's family."

The guy grinned and tapped the side of my arm. "Your daddy would be proud of you."

I hoped that might be true.

"You need anything, come inside the shed, ah? Ask for Jimmy. If I got it, you can have it. We get it done one way or another."

"Hey," I said. "You got any inner tubes?"

32
CALVIN AND BEN

One day Billy and Charlie came over with two Hawaiian guys, big as bulldozers. They were about sixteen or seventeen. Each had so much muscle that his head looked like one of Grampa's eggs on a fifty-gallon drum.

I glanced around for Little Bruiser. Charlie, for some reason, was on his good-human list, like Kimi, Mama, and Grampa Joji. But maybe not these new guys.

I stepped off the porch.

"Recruits," Billy said. "Meet Charlie's nephews. This small guy is Ben, and this one is Calvin. They're brothers. Last name is Young. Ever heard of them?"

The Young twins! Ho! They were probably the best high school football players the entire territory had ever seen. They played barefoot ball in a country rural league on the other side of the island.

"Ho," I said. "You guys play for Kahuku, right? The Red and Whites? One time you played Punahou just for fun? Right? And you won."

Both of them glared at me with their beefy arms crossed, giving me their most dangerous looks. I stepped back.

Billy, the fool, grinned.

"Nuff, already," Charlie said, elbowing one of his giant nephews.

Ben and Calvin both broke out into big white-tooth smiles and reached out to shake my hand.

"Phew," I said. "Had me worried there for a second."

"They were just showing you how mean they can look," Billy said. "Might come in handy sometime."

Surprisingly, they shook like normal guys, no bone-crushing finger-breaking grips, which for sure they had. I don't care how strong my own grip was, they could have crushed my hand like a matchbox.

"I thought you might need some help to muscle up your daddy's boat," Charlie said.

I glanced at Billy. Now even Charlie knows?

Billy shrugged.

"We can come Uncle's place anytime," Calvin said. "Just call us . . . anytime. We come help you."

"Great! You got any inner tubes?"

33
ROCKS

Twenty-three.

That was all we could dig up. Twenty-three tubes, four with big red-rubber patches on them. Depressing, but like Billy said, it was wartime, and twenty-three was pretty good.

We took them all, and some rope, down to the canal on the city bus. Five of us—me, Billy, Mose, Rico, and Grampa Joji. One lady asked if we were going to the beach. "Yeah," I said, "the beach." I didn't know what she thought Grampa was doing with the tubes he was carrying.

We stood along the edge of the canal looking down on the *Taiyo Maru*. We had twenty-three tubes, twenty-three short coils of rope, and one long one to go all the way around the boat. My idea was to spread the tubes out equally around the hull, just under the sampan's splash shield, which was five or six feet underwater. Not an easy task.

"Whatchoo waiting for?" Grampa Joji said. "Go."

I shook my head. "I don't think we got enough tubes to lift a turtle, Ojii-chan."

"Humpf."

"Try um anyway, ah?" Rico said. "It's hot. I like swim."

"Unnh," Grampa agreed, nudging me toward the water.

Mose took one end of the long rope and I took the other. We swam around the hull, leaving rope floating on the water, and met on the other side. Billy and Rico jumped in, so now we had two guys on each side of the boat and one long rope surrounding it. But of course we were on the surface and the splash shield five feet down.

"Okay," I said. "When I count to three, we dive this rope down and secure it all the way around the hull, just under the splash shield . . . you with me?"

They nodded. I counted.

We went under.

It took longer than I thought it would, but we did it on the first try. My lungs were screaming by the time I came gasping back up for air.

"Hoo-ee!" Mose shouted. "I never thought I could hold my breath that long."

"Stop smoking," Rico said, "and you could hold it longer."

"Smoking? I don't smoke, you fool."

"Yeah, but you might someday."

Mose stared at Rico. "In your mind that makes sense?"

Rico grinned and tapped his head with a finger. "Brilliant, remember?"

Grampa Joji tossed out orders. "Come, come," he said, waving us in. "No stop now."

We climbed up over the rocks that edged the canal.

The hot morning sun dried us off quickly while we sat on the bare dirt, tying the short ropes to the inner tubes, so that now we had tubes with ropes like the kind you held on to when you threw them out to a drowning swimmer.

We tossed the tubes into the water and jumped in. Now the hard part—pushing them down under the boat's splash shield. There was only one way I could think of to do it: raw muscle—since we sure couldn't take them down flat and inflate them underwater. Anyway, we didn't even have a pump.

We spread them out, eleven inner tubes on one side, twelve on the other.

"How we going push these down below the splash shield?" Rico said. He pulled himself up on a tube and leaned on his arms, floating. "Look. I can't push it under. Too strong."

"Not push, Rico. We going pull um with these ropes," Mose said. "What? All this time you thought we was going push um down? Jeese."

"Hey, what I did?" Rico said.

"Okay, listen up," I said. "First we have to stick these short ropes under the long rope we just tied around the hull. Then we come up and stand on the deck and *pull* these things down. Then we tie them off." I paused, picturing it. "Whether or not they lift the boat off the bottom is another question."

One by one, we dove down and slipped the short ropes under the main rope and came back up with the loose end.

When we were done, we stood waist-deep on the submerged deck. "All right," I said. "Start pulling those tubes under. Mose, you go down and tie them off."

"You got it."

It was backbreaking, muscle-popping work, worse than pulling up big fish from the deep sea. My hands grew raw and painful. Billy grunted and Rico complained, but we did it—all twenty-three tubes.

Which did exactly nothing to lift the *Taiyo Maru*.

Zero.

We were standing silent and beaten on the slimy deck when Rico yelped and grabbed his head.

"Hey!" Billy shouted as more rocks rained down on us.

I looked up to see Grampa Joji scurrying away to the trees.

We jumped off the *Taiyo Maru* and raced for shore, scrambling up the rocks and sprinting out of range.

But Keet Wilson and his flathead friends on the other side of the canal tried to hit us anyway.

34
PONTOONS

"Jake put an ad in the paper," Billy said four days later.

We'd taken the bus down to the canal right after school. Mose and Rico had headed home, because Rico still had a headache from getting hit by that rock. I felt bad for him. First he got shot, now he got hit with a rock. He wasn't having a very good year.

"What?" I said, only half listening to Billy.

"I said, Jake put an ad in the paper . . . for the truck."

"When?"

"Yesterday."

We were sitting in the weeds with our knees up and arms crossed over them, the *Taiyo Maru* in the water below us. A few minutes passed.

"Yeah," Billy whispered, nodding his head. He snapped up. "Yeah, yeah!"

"What?" I said.

Billy snapped his fingers. "Pontoons, that's what!"

"What's pontoons?"

"Listen," he said. "There's this kid I know over in Ka-neohe. His dad is a marine, but they don't live on the base. They live in a neighborhood like everyone else. Anyway, in that kid's backyard he had this huge black rubber thing . . . like a giant rubber float, and I mean it was as big as a car. What we did was run water from a hose over it so we could slide off it for fun. He called it a pontoon, something his dad brought home from the marine base."

"Huh," I said. "Sounds fun, I guess."

"You don't see what I'm getting at?"

"No."

"Pontoons . . . if we had two of them? Each one as big as a car?"

"Yeah?"

He grinned and tapped my arm with the back of his hand. "And, this is the key, we inflate them with something like a compressor—underwater?"

Bong!

"Man, I'm slow," I said, the picture now developing in my brain. "Ho! So how can we get one? Can we borrow that kid's? Is it heavy?"

"Whoa there, hold on, son, it's just a thought. We got to think it out. And we'd need two of them."

"Yeah, yeah. Two."

"Pontoons . . ."

"Pontoons! I like it."

"First thing is that we have to see if it's even possible to

154

borrow something like that," Billy said. "I'll call him up tonight."

"That'd be good," I said. "Since we don't have a phone."

"Right."

Billy was a good guy. It didn't matter to him that we didn't have a phone, or that Grampa slept on the floor, or that we washed our clothes in a tub behind the house. Billy didn't even seem to notice that he was a haole, and that haoles weren't supposed to hang around with Japanese.

We took the bus home, thinking about pontoons.

When we got to my house Billy raised his chin. "Later," he said. "Got a phone call to make."

"Good luck."

Billy headed through the trees.

Azuki Bean and my two homeless dogs, Shrimpy and Joe, stood at my feet, yawning. All of them were over a year old now. I wanted to keep Shrimpy and Joe and wasn't trying very hard to find homes for them. But I would have to, and soon. We couldn't afford to keep feeding them.

I dropped down on my knees and sat back on my heels in the dirt, and the big puppies nosed over to me. "You little rascals, how's life, huh?"

I rubbed their fat, warm bellies.

The screen door squeaked open and I glanced up.

Keet Wilson let the door slap shut behind him.

35
INTRUDER

I felt my jaw drop, just slightly, not enough for Keet to see but enough for me to know I'd just been hit on the head with a hammer.

I stood, slowly, brushing the dirt off my knees.

Keet glanced off to my left, and I looked that way. Little Bruiser was tied up short in the shadow of a tree. I turned back. "What are you doing in our house?"

Keet swaggered down the steps. "Whose house?"

I said nothing.

Keet humphed. "I thought so."

Mama must have gone somewhere with Kimi, I thought, the house dark through the screen door.

Keet came closer, now four, maybe even five inches taller than me. My eyes were level with the two fake army dog tags he wore around his neck.

"Where's your white shadow?" he said.

I didn't answer.

"How about your mommy? I need to talk to her. She's not in your house . . . oops, I mean, she's not in my house."

I turned to the side and spat into the dirt. I could get one clean shot at his nose before he killed me. It would be worth it.

Nakaji must always be a good name, Tomi. Only Papa's words held me back. But it wasn't easy, especially remembering the rock that slammed into Rico's head, and Grampa hurrying away, scared and rattled. What kind of sick dogs would throw rocks at an old man, anyway?

Keet reached out and placed the tips of the thumb and fingers of his right hand on my chest. He shoved me, and I stepped back, but I never took my eyes off him.

"Your room is a sad place," he said. "It's as pathetic as your life."

"You had no right to go in our house," I said.

"Oh, I have a right, fish boy." He grinned. "We own you." He shoved me again.

"Do that again and you'll wish you hadn't," I said.

"Ooo," Keet said. Then laughed. "You know what I found kind of touching in your room? I mean, besides the fact that you sleep in there with that insane grandpappy of yours?"

I waited.

Keet winked. "You saved all the pieces of those stupid fish. Cute."

Papa, this is too hard.

I headed around him and started up the steps.

"When mama-san gets home you tell her she's needed up

at the house. We got company coming, and our house—and this dump, too—got to get dressed up, know what I mean? We don't want *any* Jap symbols of *any* kind around this place, including stupid fish kites, you hear me? You tell your mama to come on up to the big house just as soon as she shows up."

I pushed past him, heading up the steps.

"Oh," Keet added. "We need her for something else, too."

I let the door slap behind me.

"I need her to make my bed!" he shouted, then laughed.

The house was empty. Silent.

I was burning up, ready to go after that dog no matter what Mama or Papa would say about it. I was glad Mama wasn't home.

But I would have to tell her.

And she would have to go over to the Wilsons'.

I checked the house, going room to room. The only thing that wasn't as it should have been was my bed, which was turned over. My special glass ball that Sanji had given me was still on the windowsill, and my clothes were untouched in the stacked wood boxes I used as shelves. But my blanket was crumpled on the floor, my pillow tossed into a corner, and the pieces of the *koi-nobori* were sprinkled over my upturned mattress.

I gathered them up carefully, then replaced the mattress and gently flattened out the pieces of red paper. There was no way in this mean world that he was going to defeat me.

Never.

Like Mr. Ramos said, if you don't fight for what you

love, you might lose it. You hear that, Papa? Sometimes you just got to do it.

I placed the fish pieces under the mattress, then went out and untied Little Bruiser and hurried away so he wouldn't charge me. But for some reason he just looked up at me, then trotted out into the sun.

36
A
WARNING

Awhile later, Mama came home from the grocery store with Kimi pulling a wooden wagon full of vegetables, a big bag of rice, and a few canned goods. When she looked into my eyes she knew something was wrong.

I'd been sitting out on the porch steps with the dogs, waiting and wondering if I should tell her about Keet. I didn't want to put that weight on her. I also knew that she would absolutely want to know about it.

"Tell me," she said.

I glanced at Kimi.

Mama took a couple of cans out of the wagon and handed them to Kimi. "Go put these away," she said softly, which made Kimi brighten with responsibility.

I got up and let Kimi go by, then went down to stand

closer to Mama. "When I came home Keet Wilson was coming out of our house."

"He was inside?"

I nodded. At my feet the puppies tumbled over each other. I nudged them with my foot and they scampered off.

"He didn't take anything," I added.

Mama frowned.

"He said his mother wanted to see you when you got home. I guess she sent him down to get you."

Five minutes later, Mama was out the door and heading up the trail. She never felt put out by Mrs. Wilson. Mama worked for her. It was always as simple as that, and I suppose that was how I should have looked at it too. We were lucky to live where we did, in a nice house, up where the island was green and cool.

But sometimes that way of thinking wasn't easy.

Twenty minutes later, Mama returned. She said nothing, and the look on her face didn't either. She just went about her business in the kitchen.

"Mama?" I said. "What did they want?"

"The Wilsons want you to dig a bomb shelter for them," she said.

"Me? By myself? Why? Nobody's bombing us anymore."

"You dig. They pay us more."

"But—"

"Go find Ojii-chan," she said.

"I don't know where he is, Mama. His bike is gone."

She rattled around the kitchen. There was more that she wasn't telling me.

Kimi came in and stood between us, looking up.

Mama didn't really need to tell me anything. It was all about me. The Wilsons didn't have guests coming. They sent for Mama to complain about me, and maybe the *koi-nobori*.

I felt Mama's confusion. To honor the Wilsons would dishonor me, and to honor me would dishonor them. It had to be tearing her up, the feelings I knew she felt, but would never reveal.

"Tomi-kun," Mama said, quietly. "You have to find your grandfather. He's getting old. He . . . we need to help him. He forgets things, and he wanders away without telling us where he is going."

"I know, Mama. I'm sorry. I'll go find him."

"I miss your . . . I miss Papa." We looked at each other.

"Me too, Mama. Me too."

"We have to be strong now. You have to be the man, help me, help Kimi, like your father would do."

I stared at the floor. Five bomb shelters I would dig if that was what Mama needed me to do.

I headed out.

I couldn't believe the Wilsons wanted me to dig a bomb shelter when they had their own son to do it and he was bigger than me. *Papa,* I thought, *come home soon. I don't know how you and Mama can just jump when they say jump.*

Lucky came out from under the house and followed me. There will be a day when things will be different, I thought, and when that day comes Keet Wilson will have to dig his own holes and choke down whatever ugly thoughts are moving around in his little mousebrain, because on that day he will lose his power over me. On that day we will be equals.

And that day was coming.

37
FRANKIE

First I checked for Grampa by his chickens, Lucky tagging along for something to do.

No Grampa.

I went over to Charlie's place, where he often went to visit.

Nope.

Was Ojii-chan losing his common sense? Always running off without telling anyone where he was going. With martial law, and with him being a citizen of Japan, it was too dangerous to be so careless, and he knew it. Worse, he never took his ID or gas mask with him. I had to laugh, trying to imagine Ojii-chan in that bug-eyed thing. Never would he put something like that on, not even in a gas attack. You'd have to tackle him and force it on.

"Go home," I said to Lucky. "Go sleep under the house."

She loped off, knowing by the tone of my voice that it was time to be somewhere else.

I headed out to the street to the bus stop. Poor dog only wanted to go somewhere with me. "Sorry, Lucky," I whispered.

Ojii-chan. Where could you be?

All I could think of was that he might be downtown with Fumi. But who knew where she lived, or worked? I didn't even know her last name, and there had to be a thousand Fumis.

I took a deep breath and blew the air out through puffed cheeks, looking up at the sky, thinking. Where should—

What's this?

Way up in the blue cloudless universe five tiny white specks circled around each other. I knew instantly what they were: *hato poppo*. Pigeons. High flyers. Like Papa used to have, until the army made me kill them. A handful of Papa's birds had been out flying that terrible day, so had survived. When they came home I gave them away so they wouldn't end up dead too.

I watched the high flyers circle against all that blue.

I blinked.

Funny how five little dots could choke me up. In that moment I remembered the day Papa and I had spread out on our backs, lying flat in the grass, watching his high flyers soar, and him saying, "Mama should see this, Tomi."

But she never did.

And then the pigeons were dead.

Where are you, Papa?

I watched the high flyers a minute or two more, then looked away. Enough. Go find Ojii-chan.

***

I got off the bus in Chinatown.

Vegetable stands, pool halls, hole-in-the-wall restaurants, streets full of people hurrying around. Finding Grampa would be like trying to find a grain of rice on the beach.

Through the buildings I caught glimpses of the bright blue ocean beyond, with Sand Island on the other side of the harbor where the temporary prison was, the place they'd taken Papa after they arrested him. I winced, remembering how I'd put myself and my family in danger by swimming out there. I hid in the weeds all day, waiting for a glimpse of him through the fence. I was wrong to do that; but I was glad I did. It was the last time I saw him.

A car honked.

I jumped back and stood on the curb. This is hopeless. Grampa could be anywhere, maybe even not downtown at all.

Tst.

Okay, check around Hotel Street where all the action is, and go home. Why am I always looking for Grampa, anyway? He's a grown man. He can take care of himself.

Maybe.

And who was this Fumi?

How come all of a sudden he's got a girlfriend? He was getting weirder by the minute. Where are you, Ojii-chan?

On my way to Hotel Street I ran into Ichiro Fujita, one of the guys on the Kaka'ako Boys baseball team, who we used to play before the war. He was pushing an old wood wheelbarrow.

"Heyyy," he said, smiling big. "Whatchoo doing down here with the common folks?"

"Looking for my grampa," I said. "What are *you* doing here? Kind of far from home, ah?"

"My job. I work now, delivery. Vegetables, mostly, from Kaka'ako farmers. Pays pretty good."

"You mean you quit school?"

"Had to. Hard for lots of families to get by these days."

I nodded. "Yeah . . . did they arrest your dad?"

"No, no . . . but they took my uncle away. He was a Japanese-language-school teacher. I'm helping his family out."

"You're a good guy, Ichiro."

"Frankie."

"What?"

"My name is Frankie now."

"Frankie?"

"Changed it. Lot of guys doing that now."

"What guys?"

Ichiro looked off toward the ocean. "You got a name like Ichiro and you got people suspicious without you saying a word, you know? Japanese names being changed all over, at least down here."

"Frankie . . . that's you now?"

Ichiro grinned. "I like Frankie. Like the president. You

should change yours." He thought a moment. "Naah. Tomi is okay. Like Tommy. Just change the way you say it, ah? Easy."

I shrugged. "I guess."

"How's that haole frien' of yours, the pitcher?"

"Good."

We stood thinking of what to say.

"Well, I got to get back to work," he said. "You stay safe, ah? Watch out for pickpockets down here."

"Nothing to pick in these pockets."

He grinned, tapped the side of my arm, and went on down the road with his wheelbarrow.

He was all right, Ichiro. Too bad he had to change his name.

Seeing him working to help out his uncle's family . . . that was what I should be doing, helping out, not chasing after my impossible idea. I should just give up and get a job.

I walked around Hotel Street for an hour, feeling low. Ojii-chan was nowhere. All I found was two million sailors, army guys, and civilian construction workers. If Grampa was anywhere near this place he'd be buried in uniforms and I'd never see him.

"This is crazy," I mumbled.

The sun was going down. I had to get home, Grampa or no Grampa.

38
MR. WILSON'S CAR

I got off the bus by the Piggly Wiggly market on Nu'uanu Avenue, not far from my house. I hadn't even come close to finding Grampa.

I hurried up to my street, daylight fading to dusk.

A car pulled alongside me, its engine humming low, keeping pace with me. I glanced over.

Mr. Wilson studied me, then braked to a stop. "Get in. I'll take you the rest of the way."

"That's all right, I'm almost—"

"Get in."

I opened the door and slid down onto the leather seat. Mr. Wilson's briefcase was in the way so I pushed it closer to him.

I pulled the door shut.

Mr. Wilson turned onto our street and pulled over.

The engine idled.

Other cars drove past us, everyone hurrying home before dark.

I felt Mr. Wilson studying me, felt his heat. In the corner of my eye I could see his belly, almost touching the steering wheel. My first thought was: Keet told him about the *Taiyo Maru*.

"I'm having a hard time justifying keeping your family on my property," he said.

I couldn't even force myself to look at him. "Yes, sir."

I waited.

"I heard about the Jap kites you had flying over your house."

Another car passed.

"They're not there anymore," I said. *Your son took them down and ripped them to shreds.*

"You can't do that, boy. I can't have any enemy symbols and emblems around my place, do you understand that?"

"Yes, sir."

He tapped his thumb on the steering wheel, both hands gripping it. "The FBI came up to the house the other day. They wanted me to give up my shortwave radio."

When I didn't say anything he shoved his briefcase into me. "You hear that?"

I jumped. "Yes, sir."

"I don't like to be put in the same boat with enemy aliens, don't like that at all, I'll tell you, and if there's just one more incident, one more symbol, or one more visit from the FBI, military, police, or even a block warden, and that incident has anything to do with you or your family, I'm cutting you loose, I don't care how much Mrs. Wilson needs your mother up at the house."

"Yes, sir."

The sky was darkening fast, the street ahead turning vague in the dusky light. Mr. Wilson didn't know about the boat. Because if he could get this mad about fish streamers, he would . . .

"You know why they wanted the radio?"

"No, sir."

"The law, boy. Things have changed for everyone, even the innocent, all because of you Japs. Now you can't keep a shortwave anywhere that an enemy alien has access to it, you get what I'm saying?"

Mama.

An enemy alien. Right, I thought—she's sending messages to Hirohito, now—*come bomb us again, was fun that first time.*

"You know what I did with that radio?"

"No, sir."

"Well, I sure didn't give it to them, I'll tell you that. I took it down to the office so the FBI could relax about your mother getting her hands on it."

I nodded.

Then got bold.

"Mr. Wilson, you think my mother would really ever even get near that radio, except maybe to dust it off?"

He chuckled. "If she ever did, it would surprise me, and it would surprise her, too, because I'd have her arrested quicker than you could turn the thing on. But that's not the point. The point is you are all an annoyance and, frankly, a

171

worry to everyone around here. Who's to say what the old man is up to? They never should have turned him loose. And you . . . who's to say you don't have something subversive going on? My son says he thinks you're up to something, but he won't say what that is. You care to enlighten me?"

I pursed my lips, afraid I would pop something off at him, and no matter how mad I got, I couldn't do that.

Swallow it. Now.

"I'm sorry about your radio, Mr. Wilson, and you won't see any more fish symbols while the war is going on, or any other symbols."

Mr. Wilson kept tapping his thumb on the steering wheel. He took a deep breath, then said, "Listen, I don't want to have to ask your family to leave. I'm a compassionate man."

"Yes, sir."

He put the car in gear but kept his foot on the brake, his eyes looking into the rearview mirror and staying there. I looked back over my shoulder at Grampa Joji coming up the road on his wobbly bicycle.

Mr. Wilson's eyes squinted down. "You tell him everything I just told you, because I'm as serious as a train wreck about this, you understand?"

"Yes, sir, I'll tell him, and Mama, too."

He turned to look me in the eye. I looked back at him, but only for a second. "Good," he said. "You can get out of my car now."

39
THE FORCES ARE MOVING

One thing was for sure—if Mr. Wilson ever heard about what I was doing with the *Taiyo Maru* he would come down on me like a lightning bolt. And even though he'd warned me to pass on what he'd told me to Grampa and Mama, I was keeping it to myself. Why bring them more worry? I would have to be more careful, that's all.

Very careful.

Billy, too.

The next day at school I told him about what happened in Mr. Wilson's car.

"He really said that? Get out of my car?"

"He shoved his briefcase into me too."

Billy shook his head. "Guy's a winner."

"Like son, like father, huh?"

"Looks like it."

We were silent a moment.

"I was thinking I should forget about the boat and get a job," I said.

"What!"

"Do more to help out, you know?"

"That's good, but—you just going to drop the whole *thing? Now?*"

I looked away. "No, I—"

"Get that thought out of your head, because you already are helping out. You're trying to save your dad's boat, remember? He needs it. I don't see how much is more important than that."

He was right. The *Taiyo Maru* was our life. It was all we had.

"Hey, I have some news," Billy said. "First, I had to tell Dad what we're trying to do."

"What!"

"Don't worry. He's not going to blab it to Mr. Wilson or anyone else. But listen to this—you remember those pontoons I was talking about?"

I frowned. Mr. Davis knew. That wasn't good.

"You with me here?" Billy said.

"Yeah. Sorry. What?"

"The pontoons . . . I learned what the marines use them for. Two things. First, they use them to make temporary bridges. What they do is lash them together and anchor them in the river they want to bridge over. Then they put a steel mesh on top on them, strong enough for tanks to cross."

"Smart idea."

"You're going to like the second thing they do with them, because it shows you how close you are to getting it right."

"No joke?"

Billy rapped the top of my head with his knuckles. "Seems you might have something in there after all, because the military also uses pontoons to bring up small sunken boats."

"Ho! Really?"

"Yep. Same idea as yours, with those inner tubes. You just did it backwards—and, as we know, you didn't have enough tubes."

"How'd I do it backwards?"

"We did it the hard way. The easy way would have been to put the air in *after* we secured the rubber to the hull."

"But how?"

"The compressor I told you about. Remember?"

"Yeah, they work underwater?"

"Sure do."

Ho . . . you could blow them up underwater. I knew what a compressor was, but how could we ever get one? "So all we need is pontoons and an air compressor?"

"I know what you're thinking," Billy said. "But don't cash your chips in yet. Dad might be able to borrow two pontoons, and he thinks that's all we'd need—two."

"I'm sorry you told your dad about this, Billy . . . what if he says something accidentally?"

"To who?"

"I don't know, but Mr. Wilson could find out."

Billy frowned. "You know Dad better than that, Tomi."

"Yeah, but it could slip out."

"Not a chance. He's on your side, remember? Always has been."

"I know, I know. That's not what I meant, it's just—"

"So quit looking depressed. The forces are moving."

"What about a compressor?"

Billy opened his hands. "Just another challenge, son."

"I got too many challenges already."

"Make a man out of you."

"Better me than you, I guess."

Billy snickered. "Hey, guess what—Jake got a call on that truck."

"He did? He sold it?"

"No, but the guy wants to come over and take a look."

"But it's still down at the harbor."

"There you go, another challenge, son. You can do it."

"Me?"

Billy gave me an easy shove. "Naah, not you. Jake said he'd tow it home. He's got to get it running first, huh?"

"Right."

"Of course I'm right."

"Pfff."

40
TATTOOS
BY
FUMI

I liked going down to Hotel Street a lot better when I wasn't trying to find Grampa Joji. It always popped my eyes and put a spring in my step, because the place was as alive as centipede legs, antsy and crawling with people. It was right in downtown Honolulu near the harbor and the big boats, and though it was called Hotel Street, it had little to do with hotels, at least not the kind of hotels I'd ever go into. Mostly there were tattoo parlors, laundries, bars, and restaurants, and girls looking good as color calendars. It was where all the military and civilian defense workers went to take a break, have a good time. Men in uniform or loud flowery shirts, some fighting and getting dragged away by MPs and SPs.

I loved that place!

And even though Mose and Rico didn't like army guys,

177

they never passed up an opportunity to go to Hotel Street, either. Billy, too.

That Wednesday afternoon, instead of taking the school bus home, the four of us hopped on a city bus and headed downtown. Last night Grampa Joji had asked me to meet him at Fumi's place. "No can miss um," he said. "You see plenny soljas line up on the street, you follow um. Take you right there."

"Ho!" Rico said. "That's your grampa's girlfriend's place?"

TATTOOS BY FUMI, WORLD'S GREATEST BODY ARTIST.

Fumi was a *tattoo* artist? "Ojii-chan, you've lost your mind," I mumbled.

"No," Rico said, brightening. "He's finding it."

"Fumi's Japanese, right?" Billy said. "I thought all the tattoo guys were Filipino."

"She's Japanese. She's just . . . unique."

Billy shook his head. "Like your grampa, huh?"

"Two of a kind."

The line into Tattoos by Fumi went around the block. In the window a sign said TATTOOS $15. Sample designs were taped to the glass: REMEMBER PEARL HARBOR, an anchor, eagles in different poses, hearts, and hula girls. We squeezed through the line of guys and put our hands around our eyes to look in the window.

Fumi was working on a navy guy in his white uniform, just finishing up an anchor on his forearm. Above the anchor WAS REMEMBER PEARL HARBOR. The sailor saw us looking and nodded with a grin.

Fumi wiped his arm with a small towel. She was dwarfed

by the big sailor. The guy checked out his tattoo, then stood up and paid her. He came up to the window and showed us his new piece of art, grinning like a donkey.

"Looks stupit," Rico whispered.

"What?" Mose said. "The guy or the tattoo?"

"Both."

Before the guy even got out the door another guy took off his shirt and jumped into the chair.

Somebody was breathing down my neck. I could smell garlic and chicken stink. I turned to look.

Grampa Joji jerked his chin toward the window. "Good, nah? *Anohito wa okane motterukara.*"

Rico scrunched up his face. "What he said?"

"He said Fumi is getting rich."

"Ho, yeah, no kidding."

She probably made in a day what Mama made in a month. But then we also got a house out of Mama's job.

I grabbed Ojii-chan's arms and checked them for tattoos, wondering if he'd added to her riches. Luckily, his papery flesh was art free. "What's this all about, Ojii-chan?" I said. "How come you hanging around this kind of place? Not like you, Grampa."

Mose, Rico, and Billy crowded closer to hear about how a cranky old goat became a Hotel Street playboy.

Grampa scowled. "You like I help you, or what?"

"*Help* me? You want me to get a tattoo?"

He slapped the side of my head. *"Meueno hitoni mukatte nanda sonotaidowa!"* he said. "No talk sassy!"

"*Ow,* what'd you do that for?" I rubbed the sting, just above my left ear.

Mose and Rico stepped back. Billy's eyes opened wider. They knew Grampa often made snappy remarks to us, but they'd never seen him strike out like that.

"Fumi wa kimae ga iihito nandakara," he said. "You no talk bad about her."

"Okay, Grampa, no problem, I know she's a kind person, just calm down."

He glared, then pulled me into Tattoos by Fumi, his steel fingers pinching my elbow.

Billy, Mose, and Rico followed. The sailors made way.

Fumi glanced up and smiled. We pushed by to the back of the tattoo shop, back through a bamboo curtain to a small room, where we crowded around Grampa Joji. I was still in shock over getting slapped, and even more by seeing my grandfather in such a place. That stockade must have changed him. Or maybe that last stroke opened something up in his brain, like memories of another life, a secret past when he was a gambler, or a criminal.

When he had our full attention, Grampa smiled—something he must have picked up way back in Japan, because he sure never practiced smiling here.

He stepped aside and swept his hand toward an oily piece of machinery on a wooden pallet.

A compressor!

"Oya oya," I whispered in Grampa's beloved Japanese. "Wow."

41
THE COMPRESSOR

"How did you get this, Ojii-chan?"

Grampa shrugged: No big deal.

"I come right back," Fumi said to the guy in the chair as she walked through the parted bamboo curtain. "I make um extra nice for you, okay?"

Fumi smiled at us. "You like it?"

"Yeah!" I said. "*Really* like it. Is it yours?"

"No, no, not mines. Your grandfather worked very hard to get that here, you know."

I turned to Ojii-chan, who grunted.

"That's where you were when I was searching for you?"

"Hnnn."

"He had to bring it in a wheelbarrow," Fumi said. "It took him two days. Slow, you know, him. First day he was halfway here. He left it at my cousin's house. Next day he brought um the res' of the way. I got him one ice cream after that."

"He ate *ice cream*?"

Fumi nodded. "Sure. He likes it."

I looked at Grampa, who never stopped complaining about American food. "Ice cream?"

He turned to look out toward the front of the shop, ignoring me.

"Who does this compressor belong to?" Billy asked.

Fumi pointed to the guys lined up on the street checking out the tattoo designs taped to the window. "What you think those boys want more than anything else? Even more than one of my beautiful tattoos?"

We all leaned to look out through the bamboo curtain.

"Money," Rico said.

"No, not money," Mose said, "what they want is some fun, take away all their problems."

"Girls," Billy said.

Fumi snapped her fingers. "That's right, haole boy. Girls. Dates. Someone to dance with, someone to talk sweet to them."

"Sounds good to me," Rico said.

Mose shoved Rico.

Rico made a kissy face.

"Ca-ripes."

"So what does this have to do with the compressor?" I said.

Grampa tapped the oily machinery. *"Onna hitorito kikai ichidai ka."*

"What?" Rico said.

Fumi put her hand on his shoulder. "I have this one customer—Bobby's his name. Oh, he's so cute and so nice, that boy. Come from Chicago. But he was lonely, too, and homesick."

"A sailor?" Mose asked.

"No-no . . . defense worker. Shipyard, Pearl Harbor. He isn't like most of those wild construction guys. No, Bobby is a gentleman—like your grandfather, Tomi—a good man."

I turned toward Grampa Joji, who smiled his crooked teeth at me.

"So I said to Bobby," Fumi went on, "I said listen, you know what's an air compressor? For put air inside car tires, like that? And Bobby go, are you serious? I use those things every day at my job. And I say, how's about you and me make a deal?"

Fumi wagged her eyebrows, waiting for us to figure it out.

"And?" Rico said.

"And Fumi told the guy you lend me a compressor, I get you a date," I said. "Right, Fumi?"

Fumi scruffed my hair. "Smart as your granddaddy, you."

I stretched a little taller.

"Bobby took a big chance letting us use that machine," Fumi said. "He could get fired if they found out what he did."

"Must have been some girl," Billy said.

"She is," Fumi said. "A good dancer, and pretty, and hoo, was that Bobby happy, because for those poor military boys, must be about hundred fifty of them to every one girl in town."

"What'd the girl get out of the deal?" Mose asked.

"Bobby."

"Not," Mose said. "The girl could just walk out on that street and she could have her pick of any one of those guys and all she got was one Bobby guy, who she didn't even choose herself?"

"Sure . . . but Bobby's special."

"How?"

"Like I said, he's a gentleman like—"

"My grandfather," I said.

Ojii-chan raised an eyebrow. Fumi put a hand on his shoulder. "That's right, Tomi-boy. Hard to find mens like this."

I would have laughed, but I knew she was right.

42
FIRECRACKER

I thanked Fumi a thousand times, grabbing her hand and shaking it. "You really helped us out, and I won't forget this, ever. I'll make it up to you someday, just ask. Anything."

Fumi winked. "Thank him," she said, dipping her head toward Grampa Joji, who was sitting on a box with his hands on his knees. "He did all the work."

I studied Ojii-chan. He was a rock to me. "Thanks, Grampa."

He nodded, quick. Anxious to get the attention off of him.

Fumi chuckled. "That old buzzard still got some moves lef' in him."

"Right," I mumbled.

"No, for real." She looked at Grampa Joji. "He prob'ly save one sailor boy's life, you know. Right outside of here, on the street. I saw it . . . that's how I met your grand-father . . . I was impressed."

All of us turned to look at Grampa, who tried to make himself be somewhere else.

"He fool you when you look at that grumpy face," Fumi said, smiling at Grampa Joji. "But inside he's a puppy dog."

"Yah!" I yelped. I couldn't help it. Puppy dog?

Grampa scowled, probably trying to translate *puppy dog* into Japanese.

"How did he save the sailor?" Billy asked.

"Five, six drunk army guys was beating up one sailor, right out there." She pointed to the street. "I was making a heart on this one boy, and I looked out when I saw everybody running over to watch in the street. The sailor tried to run, but they caught him and held him. What they were arguing about, I don't know. But *boom,* they knock that boy to the ground and start kicking him. That's when your grandfather jumped in."

I glanced again at Grampa Joji, his eyes at half-staff. Looked like he was falling asleep.

"He shout at the army guys to stop, but they no stop, ah? So Joji-san went to work. *Boom, boom,* he strong-arm two guys down. The army guys were amazed at the crazy old man, so they back off. The sailor got up and ran away. The army guys look at your grandfather and put up their hands, laughing."

Now Grampa's eyes were closed.

Sleeping.

"He's a real firecracker, all right," I said.

43
LOOKING
FOR
HOPE

The next day I was getting ready to black out the windows in the front room when I looked out and saw a Japanese woman and two small kids standing at the edge of the yard, just out of Little Bruiser's range. Like statues, they waited to be noticed, not calling out.

"Mama," I called. "Come here."

Mama came out from the kitchen, wiping her hands on a dishtowel. Grampa stayed at the table with Kimi.

"Who are they?" Mama said.

"I don't know."

We went out and into the yard. "Go move that goat, Tomi-kun," Mama said.

"Aw, really?"

"Go."

Little Bruiser eyed me as I edged around behind him and picked up his rope. He seemed torn between guarding his yard and going after his favorite target. I took his rope and tied him up short to a tree. He glared at me, then leaped. I stumbled out of range just in time. "You miserable little rat. I thought we were becoming friends."

Mama went on down to the lady and her kids.

By the time I got there Mama had a hand on each kid's shoulder and was ushering them toward the house. "Come inside," she said. "He's home."

As I followed them, the goat stared me down, waiting for the next time. "I'm changing your name to Little Rat."

Inside, Mama said, "Please, *irasshaimase*." She motioned them toward our old brown couch. "I go get him. *Shooshoo omachi kudasai*."

But the woman didn't sit. I gave her a slight bow. She bowed back but said nothing. The kids were empty-eyed and silent.

Ojii-chan followed Mama out from the kitchen. He seemed strangely younger. Must be Fumi, giving him a new life.

"Uhnn," he said, greeting the lady.

She bowed deeply.

"You were in a camp," she said in Japanese.

Ojii-chan dipped his head, yes.

"My husband, did you see him? His name is Giyozo Uyeda. He is Japanese-language-school teacher."

Ojii-chan frowned, trying to remember. In Japanese,

he said, "I don't know that name. What did he look like?"

The lady glanced at the boy sitting on the couch. "He looks just like his son. His hair is very gray, though—a man of forty with gray hair."

"Uhnn," Grampa said again, one of his favorite non-words. Then he shook his head sorrowfully. "I apologize," he said. "I have not seen this man."

The lady bowed again, clearly thankful to Ojii-chan, even though he had no news to tell her. "I had hoped you might, but thought the answer would be as it was. Thank you . . . thank you. *Ojima shimashita.*"

"*Mon dai nai,*" Ojii-chan said. "I hope he is well. And . . . if it helps . . . they did not mistreat us at our camp. And I was among good men, like your husband. We helped each other. There is little to worry about. He will be finc, I'm sure."

Tears welled in her eyes.

"Come," Mama said, ushering the kids into the kitchen. She gave a ripe orange mango to each of them, then brought them back out and wished the lady well. "Please come back anytime," she said. "My husband is in a camp too. I wish I knew how he was."

"Yes," the lady said.

"We will wait for our husbands together," Mama said.

The lady smiled, a sad smile that shared Mama's hope.

I led the small family back to the street, and as they walked away I thought of *hato poppo.* Pigeons. How they raced back from wherever they were, the island calling them home. Our fathers were pigeons. Papa and the gray-haired father would return in the same way. Their bodies would not fly like the pigeons, but their spirits would.

And we would all cry in our happiness.

44
THE BULLWHIP

The Saturday after our strange visit to Fumi's tattoo shop, Charlie clomped up our steps and rapped on the door. I answered it and held the screen door open. "Come in, come in."

He didn't. "I came to see how Joji-san is doing. He home?"

"Are you kidding? He's got a girlfriend now."

"Yeah, I heard that," Charlie said, chuckling.

"He's probably down at Hotel Street getting in trouble."

Charlie laughed. "I also heard you gotta dig a bomb shelter for the Wilsons. Billy told me."

"Yeah, but why? I don't think we're going to get bombed again."

"You never know."

"I guess."

"You like some help?"

"You don't have to do that," I said.

"Naah, no problem. Billy would come too, but he had to go pick something up with his daddy."

"Come inside," I said again.

"Naah, we go dig. We could prob'ly do um two days. Get it done fast. You ready?"

"No," I said, and he grinned. Charlie was the best.

"Yeah, I know. Just don't think how you doing the Wilson boy's work," he said, reading my mind. "Think about the big muscles you going get out of it."

"Pfff." I closed the screen door and went out back with Charlie to find a shovel. It was as good a time as any to start in on that pit. I couldn't believe Charlie would do this for me. Some people were just made to be good.

Mr. Wilson had staked out where he wanted the shelter to be, away from the house. Why did he want to build one now? The war was going well. We were winning in the Pacific.

But maybe that wasn't why he wanted me to dig it.

Maybe he was trying to keep an eye on me, or something.

Or maybe he knew something we didn't.

I thought, if we did get bombed again, I guess me, Grampa, Mama, and Kimi would just crawl under our house with Lucky and the pups and hope we didn't take a direct hit. I'd take that chance any day over being in a mud hole with Keet Wilson. They would never let us in, anyway, for sure. Mrs. Wilson might, but she had little to say in that family.

Charlie started right in, as if he were starting a new garden. Digging dirt was nothing to him. It wasn't to me, either. But when it was Keet Wilson's dirt, that made it something.

"Listen to this," I said after a couple of minutes.

He stopped and leaned on his shovel.

"I was in the Wilsons' house helping Mama a couple of weeks ago. I went up in Keet's room, just to see it."

Charlie raised an eyebrow.

"They were gone to the country for the weekend," I added. "I know I shouldn't have gone up there, but I did, and you know what I found? Our katana."

Charlie knew about that sword. He knew about everything. "Joji's one?"

"Yeah, the one I hid in the jungle until the war got over."

"Ho," Charlie whispered. "What you did? Took it home?"

"I left it there. Mama said she could be accused of stealing and get fired."

Charlie pressed his lips tight, nodding. "She's right, but . . . you lef' it there?"

"Had to."

He shook his head.

"Yeah," I said. "That's how I feel too."

We started digging again.

"You know the boy's daddy had a cousin was in the navy?"

"Mr. Wilson?"

Charlie nodded. "Was on the *Tennessee*. Officer."

I looked down at my shovel. The *Tennessee* was one of

the ships that went down in Pearl Harbor. "I hadn't heard that," I said.

"Mr. Wilson is a private man."

"How'd you find out?"

Charlie hesitated, then took up his shovel. "Ne'mind. We dig."

"What, Charlie? Tell me."

Charlie sighed, as if sorry he'd brought this up. "Couple weeks ago Mr. Wilson came over to talk to Mr. Davis about you folks."

"Us? Why?"

"He like know if he should keep you on his property. I was there with Mr. Davis. That's when Mr. Wilson told about the cousin."

"What did Mr. Davis say about us?"

"What you think? He said, Absolutely, no reason not to keep you there."

"How come you kept this quiet? I mean . . . you could have told us."

"I told your mama."

"But why not me, too?"

"Your mama no like you worry, that's all. No problem. Mr. Wilson not going do anything. Everything is fine now."

I grimaced. "Fine as a car crash."

Charlie put his hand on my shoulder. "No worry, okay?"

I nodded.

We dug.

And dug and dug.

But I couldn't get Mr. Wilson out of my mind.

Awhile later, he drove up and parked in the garage. He

and Keet got out and glanced our way, then went into the house.

A few minutes later Keet came out with the new bull-whip from his closet. He stood out on the grass where we could see him but didn't look our way.

Charlie kept digging.

"What's he doing?" I whispered.

"Just being a boy."

Whap!

Keet cracked the bullwhip. He must have been practic-ing; made that thing pop nice and clean. "Yeah, well, he's a troublemaker boy, then."

Charlie chuckled. "He jus' need something he don't have."

"What he needs is a pop in the nose."

"What he need . . . the father act like the boy not even his own son. You notice that?"

I thought a moment.

Whap! Keet looped up the whip, snapped it again. *Pop!*

"Well, I haven't seen them do anything together in a long time, if that's what you mean."

"That's what I mean. That's why the boy do stupid things. Don't matter what, just so long as the daddy notice."

I shook my head. "Doesn't make much sense, Charlie."

"Yeah," he said. "It does, you think about it."

Whap! Wop!

I tried to ignore Keet and his whip, jamming my shovel into the dark, damp dirt. "So," I said, "if he cracks that whip perfect in front of his dad, then his dad will say, Good, Keet, nice job—you sure know how to crack a whip."

195

"That's what the boy wants."

"Huh."

"Only . . . the daddy ain't going say nothing."

I nodded. Maybe Charlie was right. All I ever saw Mr. Wilson do with Keet was yell at him. Keet was always lurking around by himself. The only friend he had around our place was Jake, and Keet blew that friendship when he messed it up with Billy. Now Keet had no friends at all around here. Almost made me feel sorry for him. Sorry? I stabbed my shovel into the dirt. Not even close.

"My nephews were asking about you couple days ago," Charlie said.

"Yeah?"

"They wanted to know when you going need them for pull up that boat."

"Right now it's not going anywhere."

Ka-wop!

Charlie glanced up, then back at the pit. "That might change soon, I hear."

"You hear? From who?"

"You know Joji-san is very proud of you."

"Me? Why?"

"What you doing, using your head, trying for get your daddy's boat up off the bottom of the canal. If you do it or not, you trying. Joji respects that. Me too."

Grampa was talking about me? I frowned, but inside I felt as puffed up as a champion racing pigeon. "Yeah, well . . . thanks, Charlie, but—my inner-tube idea didn't work. Not enough tubes. But we have one more idea, thanks to the Davises."

Charlie grinned. "I heard about that, too. The pontoons."

"News flying like bullets these days," I said, starting to dig again. "That's not good, because if Mr. Wilson finds out, then that's the end. He'll fire Mama, for sure, and kick us off his land. Keet knows what I'm doing, but he hasn't told his dad yet, for some reason. But he could, and probably will."

I glanced toward the house. Keet was gone, the yard peaceful once again. Good riddance.

Charlie jammed the shovel into the dirt and sat back on the edge of the pit, now knee-deep. "Seems to me Mr. Wilson knows already."

"You think so? Why?"

"That boy not one to skip making trouble whenever he got the chance, ah?"

I thought about that. "Then you think Mr. Wilson doesn't care about it?"

Charlie shook his head. "No, I think he don't believe you can do it."

He wagged his eyebrows.

I wagged mine back, smiling.

45
HEY, BUSTA, GOOD, NAH?

I woke in a sweat.

I'd been dreaming of that bullwhip wrapping around my neck, and guns, and bombers and Keet Wilson dressed up as a U.S. Army general with his muddy boot on my throat.

I sat up and rubbed a hand over my face, my heart racing. Across the room Grampa Joji slept, his breathing raspy. Slowly, I relaxed. But it was hard to go back to sleep.

Even though we hadn't been attacked again for months, fear in Honolulu invaded every crack and crevice. We were all alone in one of the most remote places in the world. Who would come to help us? It would take weeks for ships to reach us. Deep inside, that thought spooked me. At night I dreamed of waking up to the sting of a Japanese bayonet poking into my neck.

For a while Japan controlled the Pacific. In February of

last year, the U.S. came face to face with them in the Java Sea. Mr. Ramos said it was probably the greatest naval battle since 1916, when the British fought the Germans in the North Sea. In the Java Sea we, and our allies—the Australians, the British, and the Dutch—lost five cruisers, thirteen destroyers, an aircraft carrier, an oiler, and who knew how many men.

Japan's navy was barely scratched.

Back then, Japan was using those South Pacific islands as stepping-stones, coming closer and closer to Hawaii. We were the last step before mainland USA.

But in June last year at Midway Island we broke Japan's back, as Mr. Ramos put it. If we'd lost that battle, we would all have been Japanese subjects right now.

Still, the war raged on. Men were dying in Europe and the Pacific.

And I still had terrible nightmares.

***

Later that afternoon, after Charlie and I had stopped working on the Wilsons' bomb shelter, I went out to the chicken coops with Kimi and the dogs. When Grampa had come home from the prison camp, Kimi lost her chore of tending the chickens, which to her was a sad thing. She liked the chickens, for some reason I didn't understand. They were crotchety and snippy, like Grampa. I liked pigeons a lot better, smart and clean. But now the pigeon lofts were empty.

"Maybe Ojii-chan will give you one of these chickens, Kimi," I said. "You could start your own egg business."

Kimi brightened. Knowing how Grampa loved Kimi, she might even get two or three out of him.

"I think he'd do it," I added. "You're big now, and he knows you did a good job while he was away. Right?"

Kimi nodded. "I did it just like he would."

"I know, and he knows that too. Mama told him."

"She did?"

"Yup. She's really proud of you."

"Got any eggs?" someone said.

We turned. Charlie came out of the jungle. He beamed at her. They were two of a kind, both serious about their work, both quiet and uncomplaining.

I said, "You didn't get enough digging today and want to do more?"

"Only if you like."

"Thanks, Charlie. You're the best. But I had enough already. Any news?"

"News hard to get these days," he said. He scooped Kimi off the ground and spun her around, lifted her high and set her down on his shoulders.

Kimi grabbed his head, just above his eyes.

"Hard to get?" I said.

"Police took my radio."

"Oh . . . yeah," I said, wondering why I'd never even considered that Charlie might lose his Black Zenith radio, which had shortwave, like Mr. Wilson's. "That's too bad. But why'd they take yours? You're not Japanese."

"They know I friends with Joji-san."

"Jeese, scary how much they know."

"I guess it's their job to know, huh?"

"I guess."

"Anyways," Charlie went on, "before he left this morning, Mr. Davis said to bring you over sometime around three o'clock, which is now."

"Over where?"

"Davis house. I think they got something they want you to see."

"Let's go, then."

"Go tell your mama where you going, and tell her we got Kimi, too. No make her worry, ah?"

"She's working at the Wilsons'."

"Leave a note, then."

"Right."

***

The Davises' perfect lawn rolled out before us as we broke out of the jungle, Kimi riding high on Charlie's shoulders. The sun-warmed grass, thick and fat-bladed, felt like a soft sand beach under my bare feet.

Billy, Jake, and Mr. Davis were over by the garage, Mr. Davis giving orders and Billy and Jake struggling to move something very heavy down a ramp from a trailer hitched to Mr. Davis's car.

"There you are," Mr. Davis said, seeing us. "Hi, Kimi."

Kimi smiled, shy around Mr. Davis.

Billy raised his chin, hey.

Mr. Davis put his hand on my shoulder and nodded toward the trailer. "Your pontoons . . . two of them. We borrowed them for you."

"Pontoons!" I whooped. "Yes!" I punched Billy's arm, then Jake's. I couldn't help it. I started to punch Mr. Davis, too, but he backed off with his hands up, laughing.

"Thank you, Mr. Davis," I said. "I . . . I . . ."

"You're more than welcome, Tomi, more than welcome."

"Haw!" I said, hopping around like a fool.

I helped Billy and Jake drag the first of the two canvas bulks off the trailer.

"Hey, busta, good, nah?" Billy said, just like Grampa Joji. "This Saturday we go to work."

"Those things are *heavy*," I said.

Jake snickered. "Especially if you have to carry them. You might need about twelve guys."

"Twelve?"

"Maybe more, if they're scrawny like you."

Mr. Davis leaned against the side of the trailer and shook his head. "I have to give you boys credit for dreaming this whole thing up. After all you've been through up to this point, I hope it works."

"Me too," I said.

"Sure you're up for this job?"

"I'm not sure of anything."

Mr. Davis chuckled and tapped my shoulder. "Somehow I think you just might pull this off, son."

"Hey," Billy said. "I got something else to show you."

I followed Billy around the trailer. He stopped and opened his hands toward the garage where the black Ford was, the one Jake had been fixing up. Only it wasn't the Ford in there. It was Sanji's truck.

"Ho," I said. "How'd you get it here?"

"Jake and Dad went down and towed it up yesterday afternoon."

"How'd they get air in the tires?"

"The fish place, the warehouse shed. Remember the guy said he had an air pump?"

"What about the battery?"

"Jake's recharging it now."

"About time something went right."

"What do you mean?" Billy said. "Everything is going right . . . it's just not easy."

"You want easy?" Jake said, appearing behind us. "I got just the thing, something for you two dimwits to do while Dad and I return the trailer."

He put one hand on my shoulder and one on Billy's. "I'll roll it out and you can wash it."

46
THE BUYER

"Five hundred pounds," Billy said, a day later. "That's what each of these pontoons weighs."

I was standing around with Billy in his driveway, the pontoons exactly where we'd left them the day before. In the garage, Sanji's truck was as clean as I'd ever seen it, because Sanji had never washed it once. Jake was sitting in the driver's seat, running his hand over the steering wheel. "He's falling for it," Billy said. "If he had the money he'd buy it himself."

"When's that guy coming to look at it?" I asked.

"Tonight."

I turned toward the rubberized canvas pontoon cases. "Five hundred pounds," I mumbled.

"You should have seen us trying to get these into the trailer over in Kaneohe."

I whistled. "Must have been fun. How are we going to get them down to the canal?"

"We'll figure something out. Jake drives, and he said he'd help us."

"Really? Jake said that?"

"He can be decent every now and then."

"Crazy world, huh?"

Billy snickered.

"Okay," I said. "Let's see what we got—we got you, me, Jake, Rico, Mose, and Ben and Calvin, if we can get them."

"They'll come."

"Good . . . and maybe we can get some of those Kaka'ako baseball giants."

"Them too. We're in good shape, I think."

"If the Wilson creep stays away," I said.

Billy looked at his feet. "That's a tall order."

"Hey, did you know Mr. Wilson had a cousin who was killed at Pearl Harbor?"

"Where'd you hear that?"

"Charlie. Your dad knows."

"He does?"

"He didn't tell you?"

"No."

I shrugged. "Maybe Mr. Wilson said to keep it to himself."

"Yeah, maybe."

On the way back to my house Little Bruiser popped out of the bushes and blocked the path, staring at me. I stopped. Was he still on his rope? I hoped so. I picked my way around him through the trees and weeds. When I popped out in my yard, there he was again. He trotted toward me. I would have sprinted to the house except for one thing—he was trotting, not charging. I stood my ground.

Little Bruiser came up and stood less than two feet away. Then started nubbing the weeds.

"Well, well," I said.

***

I went over to Billy's house later that evening. Me, Billy, and Jake sat out on the grass in the fading light, waiting for the guy who wanted to see Sanji's truck.

"Me and that goat got a new understanding," I said.

"Yeah?" Billy said.

"He's stopped charging me."

"How come?"

"I think he likes me now."

Jake humphed. "Maybe he's been in your yard so long you're starting to look like another goat."

Billy and I both laughed.

"Tomi," Jake said, more seriously. "About your dad's boat . . . you be careful, okay?"

"Yeah, sure . . . but why?"

Jake frowned. "Just watch out, is all I'm saying. A lot of guys at school are pretty worked up about . . . about . . . listen, this isn't everyone, for sure, but some guys still have this anti-Japanese thing going on that's kind of spooky. I mean, like Wilson? They aren't very understanding about . . . you know . . . anything Japanese, including boats."

Jake turned to look at me.

I studied him a moment. "You mean like the BMTC guys?"

"Exactly. Mr. Wilson's one of them, you know."

"Yeah, I figured that."

"Little Wilson thinks he's one too," Jake said.

"He does?"

"Sure he does. Whatever big Wilson wants, that's what little Wilson wants, and that, my friend, is a formula for trouble."

What was he saying? Did he know something he wasn't telling me? No, he'd tell me if he did. "Thanks," I said. "I'll keep my eyes open."

"You too, little brother. They got you pegged as a—"

"Traitor?" Billy said.

Jake nodded.

Billy frowned. "Fools," he mumbled.

We sat for a while in silence. It troubled me to know that all this bad stuff went beyond just Keet Wilson to other guys in his school. I scowled at the grass, my arms crossed over my knees.

Forget it, I thought. Think about something else.

"So, Jake," I said. "What did the ad say? How much you ask for?"

"Well, first I said, 1933 Ford truck, good condition, one known owner—"

"One *known* owner?" I said.

"You know of anyone else who owned it before Sanji?"

"No, but he didn't buy it new," I said. "He didn't have that kind of money."

"Still, we only know *he* owned it, so that wasn't a lie."

Billy grinned and pulled up a hank of grass.

"You hear something?" Jake said, perking up.

A car drove up the driveway, its blue-painted headlights on. Parked. A guy got out. He nodded to us. He was about Mr. Davis's age, thin with cheeks that sagged a little, and kind of startled-looking.

"Evening," he said. "I came to look at the truck. I spoke to a Jake Davis about it."

Jake pushed himself up and brushed the back of his pants off. "I'm Jake," he said. "The truck's in the garage."

We went over in a clump. The guy was dressed nicely, like he had plenty of money to buy Sanji's truck.

"Billy," Jake said, when we were in the garage. "Pull down the blackout tarp."

Billy did, and Jake flipped on the garage light. "This is it," Jake said, running his hand over the newly washed fender.

"Hmmm," the guy mumbled, walking around it, gazing at it first, then touching the paint, the seats. "How's it run?"

"Good," Jake said.

"Start her up, let me hear it."

Jake flipped off the light and nodded to Billy, and Billy rolled the tarp back up. Jake jumped into the truck. It started instantly. That Jake was a car genius, I thought. He backed it out of the garage and let it idle, headlights newly painted blue.

"Can I drive it?" the guy said.

Jake jumped out.

The guy drove it out to the street, the sound of the engine fading away until there was only silence.

"I hope he comes back," I said.

"If he doesn't we have his car."

"Oh, yeah. Good."

Fifteen minutes later the guy drove back up. He parked and shut down the engine. "Works great," he said. "What'd you say you wanted for it?"

"One hundred fifty," Jake said, cool as a businessman.

The guy nodded. "I'll give you seventy-five."

Jake stared at the guy, said nothing. Man, was he cool.

"All right, eighty-five."

"It's worth more than that, mister."

"You got papers for it? A title?"

Jake shook his head. "Nothing."

"That's a problem. Somebody might think I stole it."

Jake shrugged. "That's why we priced it so cheap."

The guy snickered. "Well, where'd you get it? You steal it?"

Jake gave him a steel-eyed gaze, and the guy backed off. "Okay, that was a joke. Whose truck is this, yours?"

"It belonged to a Japanese fisherman."

"What do you mean belonged? He doesn't own it anymore?"

"He died. We're selling it for his wife."

The guy thought a moment, nodding, his eyes on the truck. He ran a hand over the fender. "Tell you what. If this is just some dead Jap's truck, you sell it to me for ninety dollars, keep twenty for yourself and tell the wife you could only get seventy for it, how's that sound?"

Jake continued to stare the guy down, only the guy didn't seem to be aware of it. Or he didn't care if Jake was giving him some bad stink-eye.

"Now I'll tell *you* what," Jake finally said. "I'll sell it to you for three hundred dollars and tell the dead Jap's wife I could only get three hundred for it, how's that sound?"

The guy's eyes narrowed down into a squint. He stepped closer to Jake, but Jake didn't budge. "You got a smart mouth, kid, you know that?"

"Time to leave, mister. The truck's not for sale."

"How about I talk to your father before I go?"

"No need to do that," Mr. Davis said.

We all turned. Mr. Davis was standing in the darkened garage with his arms crossed. "My son's right, the truck's not for sale."

The guy crushed three shrubs and left a muddy track on the grass as he fishtailed down to the street.

47
HAULING PONTOONS

When Billy asked Jake if he could borrow back that trailer to take the pontoons down to the harbor, Jake slapped the side of his head. "What are you, stupid? What do you think we got sitting in the garage? A bicycle?"

I laughed.

"I didn't think we could use the truck," Billy said, rubbing his head.

"Why?" Jake said.

"I don't know."

"Well, now you know, so let's load up."

It was early afternoon after a half day of school on the Thursday after Jake had told the creepy buyer to take a hike. Summer vacation was just a week away. Teachers were getting ready for final exams. We had all the way until Monday to study—or bring that boat up.

Dragging those five-hundred-pound monsters into the bed of Sanji's truck was going to be a killer. But at least we had a way to get the pontoons down to the canal.

"Okay," Jake said. "Let's get this over with."

Jake pulled, Billy pushed, and I shoved those things up a wood-plank ramp into the bed of Sanji's truck, grunting and complaining all the way. Jake wasn't kidding when he said we'd need twelve guys to carry them. Made me cringe to think of that huge dirt field we had to cross, unless we could find a way to get the truck through the trees and bushes and drive them out to the canal. If we couldn't, we'd probably have to hide the pontoons until we could get more guys. One thing was sure, if we did hide them and somebody found them and wanted to steal them, they wouldn't get one inch before they stopped and said, "Forget this."

Actually, that would be funny to see.

Mr. Davis came out from the dark garage into the sun. "Seeing you boys working so hard does my heart good," he said, enjoying the show.

Billy stood with both pontoon cases at his feet in the truck bed. Jake jumped out and closed the gate. "It was nothing, old man. Piece of cake."

Mr. Davis chuckled. "Take care, all right? Drive slowly. That truck might shimmy some if you get going too fast."

"Got it," Jake said.

We headed out, slowly, all three of us crammed into the front seat.

"Your dad's a good guy," I said.

"So's yours," Billy said.

"True. I guess we're lucky."

"That we are."

This is all for you, Papa, I thought. All for you.

Jake drove through the quiet neighborhood and got as close as he could to the canal. He stopped to peer through the trees. On the other side of the street, houses slept.

"Now what?" Billy said.

"Let's walk around, see if we can find a way to drive the truck through these trees."

"I'll wait here," Jake said. "If you find something, shout."

We found a dirt road in, but it was blocked off by a chain locked to two posts. Farther on we found a place where it might be possible to drive through the trees.

"Too bad there's no road here," Billy said.

"We could make one. Just plow on through."

Billy turned and whistled to Jake.

Jake started up the truck and drove down to us, studying the bushes. "There's no road."

"We're going to make one. We'll walk ahead of you and check for rocks. Just drive over the weeds, right in here."

Jake got out and studied the opening. He nodded, got back into the truck, and followed us through. Easy. The dirt was packed as hard as a paved road.

We drove on out to the canal.

Got out, thumping the doors behind us.

Jake studied the sunken boats with his hands on his hips, whistling low. "You guys are crazy. No way are you going to bring that boat up. I thought it would be smaller." He shook his head and sighed. "This was a waste of time."

"No," I said. "We can do it."

"Uh-huh."

Gazing down on the *Taiyo Maru,* I could see his point. It *looked* impossible. Even to me, every time I saw it.

"I heard these boats were sunk by a storm," Jake said.

"Some say that," I said.

"Seems odd that they'd all go down, don't you think?"

"There's a hole in the hull of our boat. Somebody axed it."

"Huh."

Down the way two fishermen sat in the water on wooden stilt-legged chairs, fishing for mullet. No one wandered the shoreline on the other side of the canal where Keet and his fools had bombarded us with rocks.

I looked up at the sun, now heading toward the sea. "We need to hide these pontoons," I said. "Nothing much we can do today, anyway. Not enough time."

Jake scratched his cheek with his thumb. "Dad will be in deep you-know-what if somebody hauls these pontoons off."

"Who's going to take them?" Billy said. "They're too heavy."

"You got that right. I guess we can leave them here. Somewhere."

That somewhere was a patch of tall weeds in the shade of a tangle of dry trees, far enough away from where we'd hidden the boat parts that if Keet Wilson came around he probably wouldn't find it. It would have to do.

We guided Jake with hand motions as he backed the truck in. Billy lowered the gate and gazed in at the pontoons. "Can't we just leave the truck here too, so we don't have to carry these back to the water?"

"Dream on," Jake said. "Come on, twits, muscle up."

My hands had gone red and raw, and I was soaked with sweat by the time we'd dragged the two pontoons in their cases off the trailer and covered them with weeds, old brown leaves, and whatever else we could find. In the end it looked like a trash pile.

Getting them all back over to the canal without the truck was something I didn't even want to think about. But I would manage.

I shook that thought out of my head, opening and closing my beat-up hands.

48
HAMBURGERS

That night we had a rare meal—hamburgers!

Mrs. Wilson had given Mama some ground beef, something that was very hard to get. The closest I'd been to a hamburger since before the war was in the papers, when Wimpy ate them by the truckload in the *Popeye* comic strip.

"I didn't want to take it," Mama said about the meat. "But Mrs. Wilson insisted. She said not to tell her husband."

"Why?" I asked.

Mama thought a moment. "Mrs. Wilson is two people. One with Mr. Wilson, and one without Mr. Wilson."

"What does that mean?"

"Someday you will know."

"Kind of like Fumi?" I said.

She frowned. "Fumi?"

"Well, Fumi is two people too. First she jokes and bosses

around army guys at her shop, and they all like it when she does that; then on the other side she is kind and generous to me and Ojii-chan and would never think to boss us around."

Mama shook her head. "Don't tell me what goes on down there. This new Ojii-chan is too much for me already."

That made me laugh. "I know what you mean, Mama, believe me."

Mama cooked the meat in a frying pan.

Grampa came in from the chicken coops and we sat at our kitchen table, Kimi and Mama on one side, me and Grampa on the other, the windows blacked out. One light-bulb lit the stuffy room.

"These are so good, Mama," I said.

"We very fortunate, Tomi. Mrs. Wilson is good to me," Mama said, truly thankful. "We lucky to be working for them."

I looked at her a moment, then nodded. It was probably true. The Wilsons weren't so bad some of the time. We could get along.

When we were this lucky we celebrated, even Grampa, who had his own special way of putting a hamburger together, a way that I copied because hamburger and eggs from our chickens went together like mustard on a hot dog at a baseball game. There was nothing better. What we did was take two pieces of bread, slap the cooked hamburger on one piece, then a fried egg with juicy yolk on the other, then put them together. Man, was that good. Me and Grampa ate in silence, in a little bit of heaven, you could say. For once, we agreed completely.

I felt Mama's eyes on me and looked up. "What?"

She studied me a moment longer, then said, "Where you been going so many weekend, Tomi-kun? What you doing I don't know about?"

I glanced at Grampa, who went on enjoying his meal as if he weren't even in the room with three other people. But he was listening. He didn't miss a beat.

"Nothing, Mama, I just doing things with my friends."

She frowned.

Should I tell her? If I did she might get worried and make me stop, especially because of Mr. Wilson.

She eyed me, her hands folded on the table in front of her plate. "I know you're up to something. You can't fool me."

I took a big bite so my mouth would be full and I'd be unable to say anything if she asked another question. At least it would buy me some time to think.

When I didn't answer, she said, "I only want to know one thing, and then I let this go. What you are doing—would your father approve?"

I put the hamburger down and wiped my hands on my shirt, gulping down that huge bite.

"Yes, Mama. For real, he would approve."

49
THE NOTE

Early Friday morning we headed down to the canal.

Besides me and Billy, we had Mose, Rico, Jake, and Charlie's nephews, Ben and Calvin, who could probably carry those pontoons in one hand like a waiter with a tray.

"How come you don't just drive us, Jake?" I said. "We got Sanji's truck."

"Somebody might want to see it tonight. I need to keep it good and clean. I wouldn't want to chance getting in a wreck or anything either."

I shrugged. "Yeah."

"You need to think about those things," he added.

Billy snorted and nudged me. "Dad thought of it, not him."

Jake winked.

At the canal, we headed in from the street. I scowled when I saw that the weeds leading into the hiding place were flattened, and I couldn't believe we'd left it like that. We should have been more careful.

But it was more than carelessness. The boards and weeds and trash we'd covered the pontoons with were torn away and scattered all over the place.

The pontoons were gone.

"I can't believe this," Jake said.

A piece of paper flapped in the breeze, one corner stuck under a rock.

A note.

Calvin picked it up and read it silently. When he was done he looked up and grinned. "Looks like this going be more fun than I thought."

"Let me see that," I said.

We told you traitors that nobody's
bringing any enemy boat up out
of the water. It's down there for a
reason and it will stay there for the same
reason, no matter what you try to do.
So start worrying, Fish Boy, because we
might turn these things we found here over
to the police. Probably you stole them from
the army. We know your names, all of you,
and we know where you live.

It wasn't signed.

Billy snatched it out of my hand and read it out loud, his face turning pink with anger. "That's it," he said. "That moron's gone too far."

"Now we talking," Rico said, slapping a fist into his hand.

Ben and Calvin nodded, grim.

"Bad, bad news," Jake said. "Those pontoons didn't belong to us. Dad's going to—"

"I know where they are," I said.

***

We took the bus back up to Billy's house, a silent ride. Seven stone-faced guys in the backseats. Nobody sat near us. All I could think about was how creepy it felt to be robbed. Like an invasion, somebody coming in and messing with your private life. Made my stomach turn.

We stood around in Billy's yard, eight of us now, because Ben and Calvin got Charlie all worked up about it. I ran home to get Grampa, too, but he was gone. Mama was at the Wilsons', and Kimi was playing out behind our house with Azuki Bean.

"Kimi," I said. "You want a real important job? Just for an hour or so?"

We needed a lookout. We didn't need Mr. Wilson to be anywhere near his own home when we did what we were going to do. If anyone came into that jungle I wanted to know about it.

She nodded. "Something with the chickens?"

"Naah, you too smart for that. This job is bigger than chickens."

She smiled, ready to work.

With Kimi again riding high on Charlie's shoulders, we

took a muddy trail from Billy's house into the damp jungle of trees, high grasses, vines, ferns, and bamboo thickets, slapping our necks and faces at the mosquitoes.

The grass where Keet and his fools had driven their truck in was freshly flattened. We followed its trail around a couple of trees.

The two pontoon cases were tossed in the weeds with the boat parts.

Charlie lowered Kimi to the ground and squatted. He lifted a corner of a hatch cover from the *Taiyo Maru* and peeked under it, where a handful of lead weights lay in the mud.

"Keet's gone off the deep end," Jake said. "This is personal, Tomi."

"Yeah," I said. "But why, is what I want to know."

Calvin pursed his lips. "This punk needs to spend some time in jail. Look at this stash."

"Maybe we going stash his face," Rico said.

Mose frowned at Rico. "*Stash* his face?"

"Yeah, it means stab my fist in his face and smash it."

Mose shook his head.

"We better get to work," Ben said. "Where we going take it?"

"Bring it to the toolshed by my house," Charlie said. "I keep my eye on it there. Don't worry, Tomi. We watch out for you."

"Thanks," I said. "I mean that more than you know."

"No problem. You go take Kimi where she can watch for trouble."

"Yeah, yeah. Let's go, Kimi."

We crept over toward the Wilsons' house. The jungle tumbled in on us as we picked our way through the thick tangle of vines.

A five-foot tree fern, dark and leafy, edged the Wilsons' backyard.

We crouched behind it.

Mama stepped out the back door of the Wilsons' house with a floor mat to shake out. Kimi started to call to her, but I clamped my hand over her mouth. "No, Kimi. Mama can't know we're here. Okay?"

She nodded, and I took my hand away.

"Good. All you have to do is watch the house. If you see Mr. Wilson drive up, or if you see Keet or his friends, or anyone who's not Mama or Mrs. Wilson, then you come tell us quick, all right? Quick!"

Kimi's eyes grew wide and alert. "What was that stuff back there where Charlie is?" she whispered.

I hesitated, looking down at the mud oozing between my toes and around the edges of my feet. How much should I tell her? Would it scare her to know about Papa's sunken boat? As far as I knew, no one had told her about it. But she'd seen our island bombed. And worse, she'd been there when Grampa and I had to kill Papa's pigeons.

"Boat parts, Kimi . . . from Papa's boat."

She scrunched her face up. "His boat?"

"It . . . it sank."

"You mean, it's underwater?"

"Not for long," I said. "Watch the house. You know the way back to find us?"

She nodded.

I faded back into the jungle, sweating bullets about getting caught by Mr. Wilson. But also recharged by something stronger than that fear—anger.

Back on the truck path I ran into Ben, Calvin, Mose, and Rico, already heading back to Charlie's toolshed with one of the 500-pound pontoons. "Ho, you could lift it."

Calvin wagged his eyebrows.

"Better you than me," I said.

Jake and Charlie had managed to drag the other pontoon away and hide it somewhere else, just in case we got caught. If we saved anything, it had to be the borrowed pontoons, because Mr. Davis had taken a chance for us, and we all knew it.

An hour later everything but the last pontoon was stored in Charlie's toolshed. "Jeese!" I said. "We forgot about Kimi."

I sprinted back into the jungle, low branches whipping at my face.

"Wait up," Billy called.

Kimi was still behind the tree fern, right where I left her. Sound asleep.

"I guess guard duty can get boring," Billy said.

I picked her up and carried her home.

50
BUSTED TAILLIGHT

At 5:50 the next morning I eased open our squeaky screen door and closed it gently. The police hadn't shown up the night before, so I guessed Keet hadn't gone out to check his stash. Billy, Calvin, and Ben squatted in the shadows at the edge of the jungle, waiting just out of goat range. Little Bruiser was stretched out on his rope as close to them as he could get, quivering. The two pontoon cases sat on top of Charlie's four-wheeled gardening wagon—a thousand pounds of rubberized canvas.

Ho, I thought. That's what I call friends.

They stood when they saw me.

"Call off your weapon," Calvin said.

"I think he likes you," I said.

"Let's go. We been waiting since the before time."

"Handsome guys need sleep."

"Pssh."

"Jake wanted to come too," Billy said. "But he had to help out one of Dad's friends. Busted car, as usual."

"Jake's a good guy," I said.

"Someday we can debate that," Billy said.

We headed down toward the canal, the wagon creaking behind Ben and Calvin, the two of them taking turns at pulling it. Its wheels were wooden, with hard rubber around the rim. No air inside, so every time they hit a bump the wagon thumped and rattled.

"Why are you two doing this?" I said. "I mean, you got work to do at your own place, right?"

"Sure we got work," Calvin said. "But we like yours better."

"But why?"

Calvin put a hand on my shoulder. "Because you just one small, ugly cockaroach and we feel sorry for you."

I humphed and shook my head.

"Anyway," Calvin added, "we got the bug now. We couldn't quit if we wanted to, right, Ben?"

Ben frowned. "You going too far, brah. I ain't got no bugs."

"Pfff."

The streets were about what you'd expect for a Saturday morning. It was nice to be out at that time of day. It reminded me of the times I went fishing with Papa and Sanji before the war, so long ago. A lifetime. I'd give anything to be fishing with them right now, I thought. Anything.

"We sold the truck last night," Billy said.

"Hey! That's great! You get full price?"

"Better. Two hundred dollars."

"Ho, how'd you do that?"

"A crazy man bought it."

"Who?"

"My dad."

"Your *dad*?"

Billy shook his head. "Strange but true. We get to take the money to Sanji's place. His wife will be very pleased, I think."

"That's for sure. . . . Your dad bought it . . . chee. What's he going to use it for?"

Billy shrugged. "Haul stuff around, I guess."

"We should have asked him to haul these pontoons for us," I said.

"I already thought of that. Dad said sure, but we would have to wait until late this afternoon. I didn't think we had the time."

"You're right."

Cars passed, going slow, taking their time. Nobody seemed to notice us, except for one car with two haoles in it, high school guys who gave us and that wagon long looks. The car had a busted taillight, like the guy had backed into a telephone pole. They drove on.

But those two worried me, because they went around the block and passed by us again, slowly, still glaring.

"Whatchoo looking at?" Calvin shouted, picking up his pace, walking alongside the car. The car sped up, turned right at the next intersection. "You come back again, I going jump on top the hood!" Calvin waved a fist. "Stupit haoles."

"Hey," Ben said. "Just blame those two fools, we got one

227

okay haole right here," he added, tossing an arm across Billy's shoulders.

"Oh," Calvin said. "Forgot. Sorry, ah?"

"No problem," Billy said. "Those stupits worried me, too."

Calvin grinned. "Uncle said your family was good people. Now I see why. You just like us, ah? No, maybe not, because you rich. But s'okay. You helping Tomi. What other haole you know cares about somebody's Japanese sampan?"

"My dad cares."

"Yeah! Okay."

The good news was that the two haoles disappeared. The bad news was that the wagon was getting heavy, even for Ben and Calvin.

Almost two hours later we were down to the bushes that separated the last street from the dirt field and the canal. By then the sun was boiling over.

"Man, I'm thirsty," Calvin said. "Where got water around here?"

I shrugged. "In the canal?"

He slapped my head lightly.

We sat and rested in a patch of shade. But not Ben, who headed over to the worn-out houses that lined the other side of the street.

He knocked on the door of a small, rickety house with a low, rusty-colored wood fence and a gate that hung loose on one hinge.

"What's that fool doing?" Calvin said.

An old lady in a blue *mu'umu'u* came to the door. She

and Ben talked a minute, the lady peeking over Ben's shoulder at us.

"Prob'ly asking if we can drink from the hose," Calvin said. "But I never seen him wake up somebody this early."

The lady went back inside the house. Calvin turned to us and gave us a thumbs-up. A couple of minutes later the lady came back with a jug of something and a stack of cups.

"He asked a total stranger for something to drink?" Billy said.

"Looks like it," Calvin said. "Out by where we live, in Kahuku, we do that all the time. Like one big family, Kahuku. Don't matter you never seen them before. They give you something to drink, or whatever . . . they give."

Just like Charlie, I thought.

"That's great," Billy said. "Should be like that everywhere."

Ben huffed back over with the jug and the cups. "Lemonade," he said. "I told her about how we going work on one of those sunken boats today, and she said, *Oh my goodness.*" Ben shook his head. "*Oh my goodness . . .* sound nice, ah?"

I grimaced. "You can't tell people what we're doing, Ben. This isn't just any boat, it's a *Japanese* boat, and a lot of people worry about Japanese boats, even now."

Ben nodded and poured lemonade. "Yeah, yeah, okay, no problem."

We drank.

"Man, that's good," Billy said.

"She had it in her icebox for her gran-kids for when they come her house today."

"And you took it?" I said.

"She got a lemon tree behind her house. She make this stuff couple times a day, she said."

After we drained the lemonade we walked across the street to take the cups and jug back. We stood around in her yard while Ben knocked. "You boys come back anytime," the lady said. "I make more for you."

"Thank you, Mama-san," Ben said.

"Yeah, thanks."

"Thank you."

"Scoot," she said. "You go play."

We left. "Go play?" Billy whispered.

"You come back when you pau what you doing," the lady called. "I give you more."

"Yeah-yeah, we will," Ben said. "Thank you, Mrs. . . . ."

"Aurelio," she said.

"Thanks, Mrs. Aurelio."

I eased by the gate, careful not to knock it off its one hinge.

51
THE STRANGEST TIMES

We felt renewed now, and we needed every ounce of that new energy, because pulling a thousand pounds of pontoon over dirt in that wagon was a killer.

Sweat was stinging my eyes when I finally sank to my knees at the edge of the canal, the wagon on its side and the pontoons dumped onto the dirt. Calvin leaned back against them with his knees up and his arms crossed over them. Ben lay flat on his back in the dirt with his eyes closed. Billy was hunched next to the wagon looking for a sliver of shade.

For at least ten minutes nobody said a word.

Then I woke everybody up. "We still gotta take this wagon down to Fumi's place and pick up the compressor."

Billy groaned.

"At least it's not a thousand pounds," I said. "The

compressor will be easy after what we just did. Anyway, only one or two of us need to go."

"I'll go," Billy said.

"No, I'll go," I said. "I was hoping you'd unpack these pontoons and figure out how to inflate them."

Billy nodded. "That's what you were hoping, huh?"

I wagged my eyebrows. "You the smart haole, right?"

"I'll go get that compressor with you," Calvin said. He dragged himself up and turned the wagon upright. Billy knelt by the pontoon cases and started unstrapping them. Ben had fallen asleep. Mose and Rico had yet to show up.

Calvin raised a finger to his lips and winked. "Wait," he whispered, then jogged over to the weeds and bushes.

"Now what?" Billy said.

"Who knows?"

Calvin squatted in the weeds, looking for something.

Billy went back to the straps.

Seconds later Calvin hurried back, a three-hundred-pound Kahuku High School star football player tiptoeing toward us and grinning like a six-year-old.

Billy looked up.

I cringed when I saw the black and yellow garden spider crawling up Calvin's arm. The bushes were covered with those things. They ruled the islands right alongside ugly brown big-toe-sized cockaroaches.

Calvin eased up to snoring Ben and squatted next to him. He captured the spider in his fist and let it crawl out of his hand onto Ben's cheek, then sat back on his heels, straining to keep from laughing.

I rubbed my cheek. I'd hate to have that spider crawling on my face.

The spider stood still a moment, half on Ben's cheek, half on his lips. It crept slowly over his mouth, all legs working. Ben's eyelids twitched. The spider crawled up toward his eyes. Ben's snoring stopped. The spider crawled over his eyes to his forehead.

Ben's eyes popped open, crossed like a Siamese cat, and looked up at a leg dangling down over his eyebrow.

Boom!

Ben sprang to his feet, slapping at his face and hair, hopping around like he was standing on a blazing hot road.

"Ahhh!" he said. "Get it off! Get it off!"

Calvin rolled around in the dirt, laughing his head off. Ben pounced on him, shouting, "You going die for that! Your mama only going have one son after I get done wit' you, you stink-breath dog!"

Calvin couldn't fight back, he was laughing so hard. "Okay, okay. I sorry, nuff already."

"You animal!"

When they got done wrestling in the dirt, they both stood and brushed themselves off. Calvin thought that was the funniest thing he'd ever seen, and Ben, too, was okay with it, even though, he said, the only thing he hated more than spiders was centipedes.

"All right, you bazooks," I said. "Me and Calvin gotta go downtown."

"Yeah, yeah," Calvin said, wiping the tears from his eyes with the heel of his hand. These were the strangest times, I thought. There were creeps like Keet Wilson, funny guys like Ben and Calvin, friends like Billy, and generous people like Mrs. Aurelio and Fumi . . . and scary people, the block wardens, the BMTC, and Mr. Wilson. And also there were quiet times like with Kimi and the chickens . . . and a huge war raging in Europe and the Pacific, bombs still threatening to come thundering down on our heads.

All you could do was keep on trying.

52
GASOLINE

Calvin followed me into the alley behind Tattoos by Fumi. "Ho, man, this place is wild! Where all theses military guys came from?"

"Pearl Harbor, Schofield, Hickam, all over."

"Hoo, mama."

"My friend Mose doesn't like them, but they aren't so bad."

"How come he don't like them?"

"Some army guys messed around with his girl cousin. There was a fight."

"Ahh."

Trash spilled from bins behind every back door in the alley, the road black with grime. A sailor was sleeping, leaning up against the wall, his white uniform all roughed up. Calvin studied him, frowning.

Fumi's back door was unlocked.

We eased it open and went in. I could see her through the bamboo curtain, working on a sailor.

The compressor sat covered by a canvas tarp. I lifted the edge to show Calvin. "This is what we came for."

He whistled, low. "You know how to work it?"

"Not yet," I said. "Me and Billy can figure it out."

Through the bamboo curtain and out the hazy front window, you could see the long line of patient men in white and tan waiting for Fumi. By the samples she'd tacked to the walls it was easy to see that she had great artistic ability and could probably tattoo anything you wanted on your arm, or your chest, or wherever you wanted it. I prayed Ojii-chan would never go for one of them. He would look like a fool.

Out in the shop Fumi chatted with the guy she was working on, tattooing REMEMBER PEARL HARBOR on his shoulder.

Yeah. Remember.

Lot of guys wanted that one.

The sailor, a haole not much older than Calvin, saw us watching. "Looks like it hurts, but it don't."

Fumi stopped and looked behind her. "Ah," she said to us. "Come watch. I only be a minute."

Me and Calvin crept out into the shop but stayed back. It was amazing, the ink being shot by needle into the guy's white skin to the low hum of the tattoo machinery. I winced. No way I could ever do that.

"Look his other tattoo," Calvin whispered.

On the sailor's forearm was a heart with a scrolling banner running across it with the name ELIZABETH inside it.

"He must really like Elizabeth to put it on his arm where he can never take it off," I whispered.

"Crazy," Calvin whispered back. "What if he gets in a fight wit' her and they break up?"

"Every new girl going be angry every time they see it."

Calvin humphed. "He going spen' his whole life looking around for girls name Elizabet'. That's all he can do now— go out wit' Elizabet's."

"He wasn't thinking straight."

"None of these guys thinking straight, nowadays. Gotta weigh you down, ah?" He shook his head. "This war."

"My friend Herbie Okubo's brother is in the army," I said.

"Yeah?"

"Somewhere in Europe, Herbie said."

"Poor buggah. I hope he come back alive."

"Yeah, me too."

Where was Ojii-chan? He'd already left the house when I got up. I thought he'd come here.

"Okay, solja boy," Fumi said, wiping the sailor's arm with a clean cloth dampened with alcohol. "Whatchoo t'ink?"

The sailor got up and aimed his shoulder at Fumi's brightly lit mirror. "Now, there's a work of art for you." He paid Fumi and tipped her an extra two dollars, then showed off his new tattoo to the guys in line behind him on his way out into the sunlight.

The next guy, army, sat in the chair.

"Hold on, solja boy," Fumi said. "I'll be right back.

"Who's this?" she said, eyeing Calvin.

"Friend of mine, Calvin. He's from Kahuku."

"Ah, good, nice to meet you, Calvin."

Calvin ducked his head.

Just then a girl squeezed through the line of guys crowding into the shop. A silver clip held her long hair back on one side. She looked to be about my age and seemed way out of place in Fumi's tattoo shop.

She smiled when she saw me.

I blinked and looked away.

"Aunty," she said to Fumi. "Mama said to meet her at Rosie's for lunch."

"Good, good," Fumi said. "Save me a seat."

The girl glanced our way.

"These boys are Tomi and Calvin," Fumi said. "Friends of mine."

The girl smiled again, then pushed her way back through the crowd of guys. "See you at Rosie's."

She vanished.

Ho, I thought. Who was that?

"Suzy," Fumi said as if reading my mind. "My niece."

Calvin nudged me and wagged his eyebrows.

I glanced away. "Kind of hot in here," I said.

Fumi ushered us into the dimly lit back room. She took the tarp off the compressor. "You brought something for move this machine?"

"We got a wagon."

"Good, because heavy, this. That wagon can fit through the door?"

"I don't think so," I said. "Too wide."

"Hmmm . . ."

"No problem," Calvin said. "I carry um out."

Both Fumi and I gaped as Calvin picked up the compressor like it was a bag of rice he was taking out of the grocery store for somebody's grandma.

He grinned. "You like open the door?"

"Yeah-yeah," I said, and jumped to whap it open. "Thank you, Fumi, thank you."

She waved me off. "Good luck with that."

By the time we'd hauled the compressor all the way back to the Ala Wai Canal, Billy and Ben had the two pontoons out on the dirt, unfolded and ready to be inflated. When they were blown up they would look like rubber lifeboats. Along with each pontoon came a long hot dog–shaped tube that you were supposed to inflate and put in the middle of the pontoon for support.

It was late afternoon now, and Mose and Rico had finally showed up. "Glad you could make it," I said. "You two sleep in today?"

"We had chores," Mose said.

"You missed out on getting these beasts down here," I said.

"That's why we had chores," Rico said. "You got gas for that compressor?"

Dang, I thought. I hadn't even considered that. "I don't know." I found a small stick and went over and stuck it in the tank.

"Almost empty," I said.

"Now what we going do?" Rico said.

"I can get a gallon or two," Billy said. "At home."

We stood saying nothing. Going all the way back home would use up all the time we had left in this day.

Calvin checked the sky, thinking the same thing. "I guess we go home, come back tomorrow. We staying wit' Uncle again."

"Yeah, good," I said. "But . . ." I turned toward the compressor and pontoons.

"Yeah," Billy said. "We can't just leave them here."

For a moment I felt crushed. This was a big problem. We couldn't haul everything back up to Nu'uanu.

"I'll stay with them," Rico said. "No problem. Mose will work it out with my moms. I can sleep on top of the pontoons."

"You'd do that?" I said. "You think it's safe? What about curfew?"

"Forget curfew. Who going come out here? I'll be your guard dog, little man. It's warm. No need nothing, except maybe Mose might bring me some food."

"Sure, how's about I bring you a dog bone?"

"I'm not so sure this is safe, Rico," I said.

"Who going mess with me, ah?" He flexed his muscles and wagged his eyebrows.

We left with the sky turning dim and Rico lying back on one of the pontoons with his hands behind his head. Could not be comfortable, I thought. Like sleeping on a flattened out old shoe.

"Your cousin kind of lolo," Ben said to Mose as we headed home.

Mose humphed. "True, but we need more crazies just like him."

240

"He's the best," I said.

"Yeah."

"Yeah."

I shook my head. "Make that three yeahs! Rico's got guts."

53
THE
BUTSUDAN

It felt strange, dangerous even, leaving Rico down at the canal by himself. First of all, when it got dark he would be breaking martial law and could get in big trouble. But worse was the idea that we had to leave him down there at all. If life was normal, like before Pearl Harbor got bombed, then we could just go home and come back the next day. Nobody would mess with our pontoons.

But we figured nobody would be roaming around at night by the Ala Wai canal. Anyway, even if somebody did come around, Rico and those pontoons would look like a shadowy pile of rubbish.

But maybe the compressor wouldn't.

I frowned.

"Check it out," Billy said, nodding toward the Wilsons' place when we finally got back up on our street. The windows

242

were blacked out, the sun down fifteen minutes by then. Nothing looked unusual.

"What do you see?" I said.

"Look on the side of the house, just past the tree."

I squinted into the dusky light, the Wilsons' yard still as a graveyard. Just beyond the tree the back end of a black car aimed out toward the driveway, parked on the grass. The right-side taillight was busted.

"It's them," Ben whispered. "Those punks who passed us when we were taking the pontoons to the canal."

Calvin studied the car and the Wilsons' yard, the muscles in his jaw working. "Maybe I go broke the other taillight."

"Pfff," I said, moving on. "Forget it."

Reluctantly, he followed.

Lucky, Azuki Bean, and the two homeless mutts came trotting down to greet us, Lucky walking sideways as always, her flagpole tail sticking up. "Hey, Ben," I said. "You like a dog? I gotta find homes for these two. You can have one of them."

"Ho, yeah," Ben said, scooping up the smallest one. "Dusty, this dog. Stinks, too. He needs a bath."

"He's yours," I said.

"The old man ain't going like it," Calvin said. "You know him."

"Yeah, but if I tell him I going train it to be one pig dog, then he no mind. You watch. I tell, Daddy, this going be one pig hunter. He going say okay, keep um."

Calvin humphed. "Your funeral."

"I going name him Dusty . . . since he so dirty."

"You can bring it back if your dad says get rid of it," I said.

"He won't."

Billy, Calvin, and Ben with his new dog hurried through the trees to Billy's place, Little Bruiser hot on their trail. "Take that goat, too," I called.

"Hundret bucks, I take um."

"Hah!" I said, kneeling down by Lucky. "Well, that's one less mouth to feed."

The screen door of our house squeaked open. I glanced up to see Ojii-chan gazing down on me. He stood stiff in the fading light, his long-sleeved khaki shirt buttoned to his neck. His head was freshly shaved and shiny.

With slow, deliberate, boastful steps he came down off the porch.

I stood and took a step back. Something was on his mind.

"Come," he said in Japanese. "Little more light, still yet."

Not much, I thought. "Where, Ojii-chan?"

He didn't answer.

I followed him through the weeds into the trees, then into the jungle. He walked fast and steady for an old man who had supposedly suffered as many small strokes as he had. The faker was humming, too, softly singing *"Kimigayo,"* the Japanese national anthem, slow and mournful.

"Where we going, Ojii-chan?"

But he just kept on humming.

We cut through a dense thicket of bamboo and broke out to a patch of yellow ginger. Grampa waved his hand: little bit more.

We stopped in a place so well camouflaged no one could ever know it was there—a dome of bushes, with a tunnel leading into it. Inside was like being in a tent. What was this?

Grampa crabbed his way in and sat cross-legged, nodding for me to do the same.

For a long, uncomfortable moment we sat. He studied me, staring into my eyes, unblinking.

"What, Ojii-chan?" I finally said.

He leaned over and removed some sticks that were lashed together so intricately they blended into the rest of the brambly wall, completely hiding what lay in the small dark cave beyond. He reached in and brought out the black lacquered *butsudan,* the small Japanese altar he kept in memory of his wife, my grandmother, who died long ago in Japan.

"So this is where you hid it," I said.

Grampa set the *butsudan* between us on the dry dirt. He opened the doors to a photograph of my grandmother and a small dish. He placed a pebble of incense in the dish and struck a match.

We both sat silently, and the sweet-smelling smoke rose like a serpent in the still, secret cavern of sticks in the jungle.

Grampa hummed, tunelessly, now thinking or dreaming. Remembering.

I jumped when he suddenly spoke.

"This is your grandson, Okiko-chan," he said in Japanese. He spoke clearly and precisely so I could understand, knowing that my Japanese was as poor as his English.

He let a moment go by.

This is your grandson.

"You can be proud of him."

I nearly stopped breathing. *Never* had I ever heard Ojii-chan utter even a hint of praise—for anyone.

Ojii-chan closed his eyes and began humming *"Kimi-gayo"* again, rocking slowly, the incense taking him back to the land of our ancestors, where honor was everything and shame was worse than death.

You can be proud of him.

54
RICO

I got up early again the next morning.

And so did Grampa. I thought he was getting ready to come along to boss us around and was about to complain. But after what he said about me last night what could I do? Anyway, it would be funny to see him crank out orders to Ben or Calvin, or Rico, even. They would probably jump at whatever he said, respecting their elders as they did.

It would be a relief to have him making the decisions, not me.

I went outside, holding the screen door open for Grampa. But he didn't come out, so I eased the door shut and creaked down the steps and stood waiting in the dark. I looked back at the house and saw the silhouette of Ojii-chan watching me through the screen.

Moments later, Billy, Ben, and Calvin showed up. A coil of rope hung over Ben's shoulder, looking like enough to tie up five boats.

"You got out of going to church?" I asked Billy.

"Just this once, Mom said."

I nodded. "Go twice next week."

Billy chuckled, then added, "We have a problem."

"What?"

"I can't get any gas for the compressor."

I winced. "That's not good."

We stood silent a moment, thinking.

"Never mind," I said. "We can figure that out later. We gotta go check on Rico."

"Yeah, I've been thinking about him," Billy said.

I turned back to see if Grampa would follow or say something or start giving orders or what. But he stood motionless behind the screen, like a statue. Spooky. He turned and faded back into the darkness of the house.

"Let's get out of here before he follows us," I said.

"He wouldn't do that," Billy said.

"You remember when he used to wash his Japanese flag in the stream?"

Billy snorted. "Yeah, I remember."

"Guy like that could do anything, and most of it will be weird."

"You're right. And speaking of weird, listen to this—you know Sanji's truck that my dad bought?"

"What about it?"

"He gave it to Jake."

"What?"

"Jake was speechless for the first time in his life. Dad tossed him the keys and said, 'Keep it, you earned it,' and Jake said, 'What'd I do?' and Dad said, 'You became a man in my eyes when you stood up to that ignorant fool who tried to bribe you, and a man like you needs wheels, so you just keep those keys, son.'"

"Wow," I said.

"Jake said he'd drive us down to give the two hundred dollars to Sanji's wife."

"Amazing."

"Sure is."

"Funny how Jake used to be friends with Keet," I said. "And now Keet's a punk and Jake's almost a hero."

"Hold on, son, because now you've gone too far."

"Whatchoo punks talking about?" Ben said.

"Nothing much," Billy said.

"Strange ducks, you two."

"Prob'ly," I said.

When we got down to the quiet neighborhood by the canal, the sun was burning up everything in its path. It wasn't even eight o'clock yet. Mose showed up at the same time we did, carrying a bag. "Breakfast for the guard dog," he said.

We headed for the trees.

"Wait a minute," Ben said, as if remembering something. He pulled a screwdriver and a long screw out of his pocket and held them up.

"Hold this rope," he said, jerking it off his shoulder. I staggered under its weight. "Jeese."

Ben grinned, then jogged across the street to the house

where the nice lady had given us lemonade. He knelt down on one knee at the broken gate. Took about two minutes to fix the hinge, and the gate was as good as new. Ben tested its swing. Perfect.

He ran back. "Okay, let's go."

He took the rope off my aching shoulder.

When we broke out onto the field of dirt we saw Rico sitting with his knees up, facing away from us, looking at the canal. The pontoons lay right where we'd left them, and the wagon and the compressor, which I knew was as big a relief to Billy as it was to me, because I sure wouldn't want to tell Mr. Davis or Fumi that we'd lost any of it.

Mose whistled at Rico, letting him know we were there.

Rico didn't turn around.

"He got mud in his ears, or what?" Mose said.

We headed toward him. "Hey, Rico!"

Still no response.

We surrounded him. Ben dropped the rope.

Rico kept his steady gaze on the water in the canal. His eyes were puffed up and bloodshot.

Mose set the bag down and squatted in front of Rico. "What happened?"

Rico blinked, seeming to notice Mose for the first time. "Oh, you came back."

"Rico . . . you okay?"

Something bad had happened. I felt sick.

Rico gazed up at us, his eyes so puffy they were lost

in his cheeks. Yellow bruises splotched his neck and arms.

"Rico," Mose said again, nudging his cousin's knee gently.

"They came nighttime," Rico said. "I don't know when. I was asleep. It was real dark."

"Who, Rico?" Mose said. "Those same punks?"

"They didn't expect to see me here. They were surprised. Two guys. One was the punk live by Tomi. I know because after they jumped on me and kick me and hit me with their sticks, that punk got up in my face real close and said, 'You don't give this up right now you going have one war on your hands.'"

"War?" Calvin said.

"How's my face, Mose? Look bad?"

"Naah . . . you just as ugly as before."

"Rico, Rico," I said. "I'm so sorry."

Rico tried to laugh but winced. "S'okay."

"Is anything broken?" Billy said.

"Naah. But maybe something broke in the face I wen' smash. I don't know whose, but somebody not feeling good today."

Mose stood and helped Rico up. "Come. I take you home, get you cleaned up."

"No, I going stay. I'm fine. I seen worse."

"Yeah?" Mose said. "When?"

Rico didn't answer but turned and waved toward the pontoons. "They wen' cut um," he said. "They stab the pontoons. One stab each. No good, now."

"What!" Billy said.

We dropped down on our hands and knees, me, Billy, and Calvin.

"Here's one," Billy said.

It wasn't that big, couple of inches, the width of a pocketknife blade. And it didn't go all the way through and puncture the other side of the deflated pontoon. The canvas-rubber material was strong, made to resist puncture wounds. Still, it was a hole, and it would keep us from inflating the pontoon.

Calvin found a similar hole in the other pontoon, then one each in the long cylindrical tubes that went with them.

"Tst," Billy muttered.

My whole body sank back into itself, as if I were shrinking up. I felt lost, finished, dead and gone. "It's over," I whispered. "That's it."

The canal's brown water moved steadily toward the sea. There was nothing more to do but drag the stabbed pontoons home and face what trouble was waiting for us.

"It ain't the end of the world, brah," Mose said, squatting down and looping an arm over my shoulder.

I couldn't talk.

"We can fix um," Rico said, his voice drifting off.

"With what?" I said. "Bubble gum?"

Silence.

I'm sorry, Papa.

Calvin smacked his fist into his other hand. "I going hunting for white meat. This we should have done before."

252

"No, Calvin," I said. "We can't. Even now, we can't."

Calvin pursed his lips. "Only for you, I going hold back. Only for you." He punched his palm again. "Man, I like poke out that punk's eyeballs."

Papa, I'm sorry.

55
CONFONNIT

Mose tapped my arm with the back of his hand.

I turned to look back and saw Grampa Joji wobbling across the dirt field on his creaky old bike. Hanging from the handlebars were two pairs of bamboo goggles and, I could hardly believe, a gas can.

"Unnh," he grunted, riding up and stepping off the bike. He handed me the can. "For the machine."

I took the gas can and stared at it. Two gallons of gasoline for the compressor! "Where'd you get this, Ojii-chan?"

"Ne'mind," he said. He slipped the goggles off the handlebars and tossed them to Mose. We'd forgotten to bring them.

"Thank you, Ojii-chan," I said. "You've . . . you've done all you can . . . but it's too late. It's over. Look."

I showed him the stab wounds in the pontoons.

Grampa sat down on his heels and ran his rugged fingers over them, inspecting them closely.

Just when I had all the pieces—pontoons, air compressor, fuel, rope, and muscle—just when we had it all . . .

Grampa stood and headed over to the case the pontoons had been packed in and held up something none of us had noticed—a patch kit.

"Hah!" Billy said.

"Ojii-chan!" I ran over and snapped it out of his hand. "You're a genius. How come we didn't see this?"

Grampa grunted. "Army not going have this raf's without some way to fix holes, nah?"

"You're right, Ojii-chan, of course."

"Unnh."

"Okay, okay," I said kneeling over the patch kit, so excited my fingers trembled. Grampa stood back as everyone else crowded in, bending over with hands on their knees, looking at his miraculous discovery.

"What do we have?" I said. "Rubber cement, valve caps, metal roller, scissors, some kind of scratcher brush, and some patch fabric." I looked up. "Anybody know how to do this?"

"Not me," Ben said. Calvin shook his head, no.

"Are there any instructions?" Billy said.

"Not that I see."

"Confonnit," Grampa spat, shouldering his way between Ben and Calvin, a Chihuahua shoving bulls.

I got out of his way.

"J'like you fix bike tire," he said. "Look."

Mose and Rico grinned, enjoying Grampa Joji's

crankiness, which they knew so well. His ancient hands went to work, calm and steady. He found the first hole and, with the scratchy brush, roughened up the surface around it.

"Gimme one rag," he said.

We checked around us. Nothing. "Here, Grampa," I said, pulling off my shirt. "Use this."

He took a corner of the shirt, opened the gas can, and dabbed a few drops of gas out onto it. With the gas-soaked shirt he washed the roughened area around the hole. When it was clean, he stood. "Go—you got something else for do?"

I tapped Billy, feeling the smallest relief that somebody other than me was doing the bossing. "Let's figure out how we might use that rope to lash the pontoons to the boat."

"I've been thinking about that," he said.

What we had rolled out on the dirt were two twenty-five-foot floats. PNEUMATIC FLOATS was painted on them in white. When they were blown up they'd look like long life rafts about seven feet wide.

"So, Tomi," Calvin said. "We going use all of this, or just the long tubes for bring that boat up?"

I squinted at him. I hadn't thought that far yet. "Well . . ."

"I've been thinking we could do it with just the tubes," Billy said. "One on each side of the hull."

Sounded good to me. "If it fails, we add the big ones."

Everyone nodded, yeah-yeah.

Billy uncoiled the rope. "Rico, take one end and walk away from me. Let's see how much we have to work with."

Rico took the end of the rope and hobbled away. I felt so guilty about him taking that beating. He looked terrible, but he didn't seem to care. Those weren't bruises on his face, they were Purple Hearts.

Billy rubbed his chin, studying the rope. "Should be plenty. We loop it around one end of one tube, run the rope under the stern like a sling, loop it around a tube on the other side, then sling it under the bow, back and forth, securing them together."

"Then pump them up," I said.

"Hoo," Mose said. "I don't know. . . ."

"Hey, busta, good, nah?" Grampa grunted, sitting back on his heels, gazing down on his new patch.

We walked over to inspect his work, a rectangle of repair fabric solidly glued over the knife hole. I knelt down and ran my hand over it. "Wow, Grampa, nice job. You think it will hold?"

Grampa studied me, sucking his teeth, telling me without saying a word that of course it would hold and if I asked again he might have to crush me and wrap me up in old newspaper.

"Okay," I said, holding my hands up in surrender. "Now let's patch those tubes."

56
COURAGE

Except for the white clouds sitting still over the mountain-tops, the sky was as clear and blue as the sea. The sun poured down hot.

"Anybody got any money?" Rico said just past noon, wiping the sweat off his face. "I getting hungry."

We dug around in our pockets and together came up with two dollars and nineteen cents. Again I hadn't thought ahead. First I forgot to bring water, and now only Mose had thought to bring Rico something to eat.

"Sorry, Rico," I said.

"Got enough for some rice ball," Ben said. "Couple each."

Grampa grabbed the money. "Go work," he said. "I get um."

He wobbled away on his bike, heading toward the street.

"Your grampa's a nice old guy," Calvin said.

"Yeah," I said.

"Look at him, going to buy us lunch."

"Uncle said your grandpa was an honorable man," Calvin said.

"Charlie said that?"

"He said your grandpa brave, too."

"That's what Fumi said. Feel like I hardly know the guy, and he's my own family."

"You heard about him and Chun Hoon store?"

"Chun Hoon?"

"Your grandpa. You heard that story? Uncle told us, ah, Ben?"

Ben nodded. "True, Tomi. Listen. They was down Chun Hoon store, little bit before Pearl Harbor time. Uncle and your grandpa. Uncle was grocery shopping. Your grandpa went with him for something to do."

"You never heard this?" Calvin said.

"Never."

"Huh. I guess he too shy to tell you."

"Shy?"

"Okay, proud, then."

"Proud. I can buy that one."

Ben tapped my arm. "Listen to this, while they was shopping a crazy guy came in the store waving around a machete, drunk, or maybe just nuts, ah? So the guy tried to rob the store with that machete. The Chinese man behind the counter tried to shoo the guy away with a broom, refusing to give him any money, and the crazy guy hack at him with the machete."

"Almost took the guy's arm off," Calvin said.

"The Chinese guy fell down, too shocked to cry out," Ben said. "But Uncle saw it all, was coming up on the wild man from behind—"

"But the crazy guy heard him and turned around with that machete above his head," Calvin broke in. "Uncle stopped cold when he saw that, then the crazy guy flew at him ready to take off Uncle's head!"

"Boom!" Ben said. "Just before he come down on Uncle with that blade, your grandpa streak in like a bullet and grab that guy's wrist and rolled and took the guy down and came up standing with the guy's machete in his hand."

"Ho!" Rico said.

"No kidding. The crazy guy stumble out the store and was caught later by the police. But Uncle would be dead if it wasn't for your grandpa, Tomi. He knows some kind of judo or aikido or karate or something. Got to be, ah?" Calvin shook his head, pausing.

Ojii-chan?

Saved Charlie's life? Ho.

Was courage something you could inherit from your family?

I sure hoped so.

57
IMUA!

The pontoon tubes were perfect for what we wanted to do. Each had two sets of handholds on either side, for carrying, and we used them to run the rope through.

"Calvin," I said. "You and Ben take that tube. Mose and Rico, you take this one. Me and Billy will run the rope under the stern and bow. That make sense?"

"You forget we Hawaiian, Japanese boy," Calvin said. "We know boats like you know rice."

"Hey," I said.

Calvin grinned. "We go. Jump in."

The six of us dragged the two deflated pontoon tubes over to the rocky edge of the canal and dropped them into the water.

Mose and Rico jumped in and swam one of the tubes

around to the port side of the boat. Calvin and Ben worked the other tube to the starboard side.

"Okay," I said. "Now push them under. Me and Billy will tie them off."

It was like somebody's birthday party out there, yakking and shouting, having a good time trying to sink those tubes. Ben and Calvin forced theirs under pretty quick. But Mose and Rico had to stand up and jump on theirs to make it sink.

Billy laughed. "I guess Mose and Rico need some man-sized help. You ready?"

"Let's go," I said, and we each grabbed a pair of goggles and jumped in. The rusty water was warm and tangy.

The four of us struggled the port side tube down past the old inner tubes, all of them still there, and still tight with air.

Billy and I came up gasping.

"Let's . . . tie . . . them off," I said.

Mose popped up, took a big gulp of air, then went back down to hold the pontoon tube in place while Rico came up for air.

"Ready," he gasped.

Billy and I dove under. I grabbed the rope and secured it through a strap on the front end of Mose and Rico's tube. Billy got the one on the other end. Since the boat was sitting on the muddy bottom we couldn't sling the rope under the hull. But there was enough sling space on both ends where the hull curved upward.

We swam the rope around and lashed the ends through the canvas handholds on Ben and Calvin's pontoon, tightening the rope a bit, just enough to hold the tubes in place.

Later, when we inflated them, we would have to adjust the rope as the pontoons fattened.

When the tubes were secure, Calvin glided over the *Taiyo Maru* and stood hip deep on the deck. "If this works, and we get the hull off the mud, then what? How we going drag um away?"

This part of the plan wasn't completely clear to me yet, because now I was making it up as we went along. "Well . . . what I thought was . . . we could . . . we could take some rope and pull the boat toward the ocean from the side of the canal, you know, pull it like a mule, and we could keep it from hitting the rocks with a pole."

Calvin frowned. "Maybe. But better if we had a boat that could pull it."

"Yeah, but who has a boat?"

"Look," Ben said. "Lunch."

Starving Rico raced for shore just as Grampa Joji rolled up on his bike with enough rice balls for three each, and a fourth for Rico, and man, were they good.

"Thanks, Ojii-chan," I said.

"Yeah."

"Yeah, thank you, old man."

"Unnh."

We all sat licking our sticky fingers and looking at the *Taiyo Maru,* the sun burning down like a Big Island branding iron. I turned to Grampa. "You know where we can get a tow boat, Ojii-chan?"

He scowled at me.

I turned away. I didn't think so.

Mose stood and stretched. "Let's get that pump going."

"After we get the boat up," Mose said, "we still going need one more rope for pull um, ah? Where we going get that?"

I was out of answers.

"Ne'mind," Ben said. "We swim. We push it, pull it, kick it, slap it, whatever. We not sissies, brah. We go! *Imua!*"

Rico raised a fist. "Charge!"

58
MAN
TO
MAN

While we clumped around the air compressor, they came in five cars, parked on the street, and ghosted through the trees and weeds.

One by one we looked up.

Five, eight, ten, fourteen . . . fifteen mean-looking haoles.

And in the front was Keet Wilson, walking stiff and straight, leading his thugs to war.

Grampa Joji picked up his bike and pushed it away. He passed right through the gang of trouble and vanished into the trees.

No one even glanced at him.

Ben cracked his knuckles.

Rico balled up his fists.

Calvin stood tall, arms crossed, chin high.

Waiting.

I felt my skin crawl, my tongue dry with fear. I had promised Papa I'd never scrap in the dirt like a dog. But to run would be more shameful than to fight, not only for me, but for my whole family.

The six of us spread out.

Keet and his bodyguards headed our way.

Nine had baseball bats. Six took up as much space as Calvin and Ben. Dwight had a black eye. Probably who Rico hit last night.

"Lunchtime," Calvin said.

In that instant I knew how this would go down. "We not going fight them, Calvin."

"Whatchoo mean, brah? We going crush um."

"Keet won't fight without backup. He's a coward. You have to get him alone. If I can make it about me and him—"

"Naah," Calvin said. "He ain't going shame himself in front his guys like that. You watch. Let um come. I got a big appetite."

"Let me try my way first."

"Yeah, but after that, we going eat, ah?" He grinned.

The haoles spread out in a half circle, capturing us with our backs to the canal. How did Keet have the power to get all these guys on his side? What was he telling them? Were these the guys Jake had warned us about, angry sons of the BMTC?

Keet came up, his cold eyes fixed on mine. He stopped a couple feet away, still walking kind of stiff. What was that all about? He thinks he's Genghis Khan?

"We came for my rubber boats," he said, almost friendly, as if he'd just stopped by.

Ben cracked his knuckles again. Keet didn't even seem to notice him.

On the other side of me Rico stepped up. He spat in the dirt. "Come on, punk," he said to Keet. "Right now, you and me."

Keet shifted, looked back at me and moved closer. His left eye twitched. "Later, chimp," he said to Rico, but looking at me. "First I got business with the fish boy."

"Chimp?" Rico was ready to explode.

I put up my hand. "I'll handle this, Rico."

Keet scoffed.

The others stayed where they were, blank-eyed. It was hard to read haoles. Were they worried or just crazy? These guys could scare you out of your skin if you let them. The trick was not to let them.

Keet stood so close I could feel his heat. Small bubbles of sweat peppered his upper lip. "You stole this stuff from my yard," he said. "I want it back."

"You got that backwards," I said, almost in a whisper.

"What?"

When I didn't answer, he sighed. "Now, I ask you, is that right? To accuse me like that?"

I could land one good pop right there on that sweaty lip. Maybe I could break his nose. So what if I got killed? It would be worth it. *Like dogs, Tomi,* Papa's words whispered. *Don't shame us.*

I kept my eyes on Keet's. No way I can let him think he has me at his feet.

Keet grinned. Did he believe I would never challenge him, because of Mama's job? His grin vanished when Calvin headed over to the biggest, nastiest-looking guy in Keet Wilson's army.

Keet's eyes shifted that way.

Calvin got right up in the guy's face. They stood eye to eye, and if looks could kill, both of them would soon be pushing up weeds.

"We meet again," Calvin said.

The guy glared right back. "Looks that way."

"But this ain't no football game, ah?"

The big haole smirked. "I thought you lived out by Kahuku."

"I do."

"Then how come you're here with these punks?"

"Hey, hey, hey," Calvin said. "You talking about my friends. You sure you want to call them punks?"

The big guy put his hands up. "Fine, your *friends,* then. But how come you're here, man? Wilson said there was some kind of Jap sedition going on down here. That's why we came."

"Sedition, huh?"

"Yeah, sedition."

"You know what that means?" Calvin said.

"Of course. Do you?"

"Sure, it means you might be stupid." Calvin swung his hand back toward the canal. "See those sunken boats?"

The guy stretched his fat neck to look. "Yeah, I see them."

"We going bring one up."

"Why?"

"Belongs to a friend of mine."

"Hey!" Keet said. "We didn't come here to have a picnic."

The big guy put up his hand. "Hang on a minute, Wilson—so, okay, you're bringing a boat up. What else?"

"Nothing else. Just the boat. Belongs to his dad," he said, hooking a thumb toward me.

The guy scowled and turned to Keet. "What's going on?"

"The boat, you fool, the boat! They're bringing it up so they can use it to take fuel out to the enemy."

The guy squinted at Keet, probably wondering if he should kill him now or later for calling him a fool. Slowly, he turned back to Calvin. "Is that right?"

Calvin chuckled. "If you believe what he said, then you really are a fool."

The guy looked again at Keet, then back at Calvin. "Show me the boat."

"Hey, come on, man," Keet said. "This is stupid."

"The boat," the big guy said.

"Sure," Calvin said. "Follow me."

"Wait, wait, wait," Keet said. "Get back in line."

Ho! Big guy *really* didn't like that. Keet caught his mistake. "I mean . . . just wait a minute, let me finish this. We can't let them do this, this . . . this boat thing . . . not after what the Japs did to us at Pearl Harbor, and in case you didn't notice, that's a Jap boat."

The big guy glared at Keet for a long moment, peeling

away his skin with razor-blade eyes. Then he turned back to Calvin. "What do you care about this boat, anyway? I thought Hawaiians hated Japs, just like us."

"That what you thought?"

The guy crossed his arms.

"Huh," Calvin said. "Well, guess what? Like always, you wen' sign up with the wrong side."

The guy shrugged.

"Just so you know before I mess you up," Calvin went on, "it's a small fishing sampan, that's all." He motioned toward me. "All he going do is fix um up for when his daddy come home. I just want you to know what you going get hurt for. That's all. We no more need talk."

The guy thought that over, his eyes slits in the sun.

"Now, just wait a minute," Keet said, friendly-like, which was smart. "I know we can settle this peacefully. That's what my dad always says, you know? Try to reason with your opponent. Get him to see things your way. If that fails, well . . ."

The big guy and Calvin waited.

Keet turned back to me. He wanted *peaceful* like I wanted to take eggs to his house.

Ben, Billy, Mose, and Rico closed in.

Keet smiled, his fake dog tags glinting in the sun. "Listen. I'm going to give you a choice . . . let's see . . . number one, you could, uh, die. Or you could go home . . . without my rubber boats, of course, because there's no way anybody's letting you get that fuel boat back up. You got to know that. Right?"

"It's a fishing boat."

"Yeah, well, that's what you say."

"That's what I say."

Keet shook his head. "My dad says sooner or later with the right kind of . . . persuasion . . . every opponent eventually comes around."

"Well, your daddy's not here, is he? And I'm not coming around to anything! *You* are."

Keet fake-frowned. "What does that mean?"

I leaned closer. "It means we going settle this. Right here in front of all these guys."

Keet's eyes slipped one way, then the other.

"Not a chance," he said, still cool. "You think I'm going to give you such an easy way out? Give you a little beating and go away?" He chuckled and glanced back at his army.

Silence.

Keet sobered up. "You think you're pretty smart, don't you?"

"Smart enough."

"Huh."

I glared at him.

"Well, I got something that might change your mind."

He reached up over his shoulder, down behind him, his ice-eyes on mine. Slowly, slowly—he came up with a long blade that gleamed in the sun.

A silver sword.

I gasped, my jaw dropping. "Wha—"

Keet grinned, holding up my family's katana, the shiny blade pointing to the sky. "You like my toad sticker?"

I stepped back, my heart a hammer in my chest. Something

like whirling dust bobbed in my eyes and hate rushed over me like never before.

"I thought you might recognize this."

He turned the katana slightly so the sun's reflection snapped in my eyes and made me squint. The blade was so close I could see where his greasy fingers had smudged the silvery steel, and the small knick the .22 had made when Keet shot it in the jungle. "You—you can't—"

"Shut up! Now, you listen to me." He glanced down the line of guys, everyone watching. I stood ready to hit the ground if he swung the blade. That was what he'd brought it for. It would cut deep. I stepped back, sweeping away the sweat dripping into my eyes with the back of my hand.

Keet lowered the blade, angling the point down to the dirt at his feet so that it crossed his body from right to left. Then he raised his foot and rested it on the steel. "I could step on this and break it, easy," he said. "But even if it's too strong to break it will bend. Either way it's ruined."

"Don't! That's—"

"Listen close," he said. "You're going to do exactly what I say. Get the picture?"

All eyes were on Keet.

He pushed down on the blade, lightly. "See it bend?"

"You can't do that!" Billy said. "That sword's—"

"Shut up!"

Billy shouted, "That sword's been in his family for hundreds of years!"

I clenched my teeth, ready to lunge, waiting for a break

in his concentration. It had to be timed exactly right. His foot had to be off the blade.

"You know what's wrong with you, Nakaji?" Keet said. "You're a coward, afraid to fight. You've been like that forever—talk big, but under your skin you're nothing."

"You stupit haole," Rico said, starting toward him.

One of Keet's guys blocked him. Rico shoved him, but the guy didn't budge. When Rico tried to go around him, the guy shoved Rico back.

"Wait!" I said. "I can . . ."

I can what?

"See?" Keet said. "A coward. Only your monkeys stand up for you. And like you, they're nothing."

Keet moved his foot off the blade, then put it back, making me sweat.

He gritted his teeth and stepped down, hard.

"No!"

I hammered my fist into his mouth.

He reeled back. The katana fell from his hand. Billy dropped to his knees and grabbed it, then scrambled up, took it behind Ben.

Keet staggered, blinking. He charged me.

I ducked his flailing fists and hammered him just above his eye. He roiled back.

A dog in the dirt! That was me.

He swung again. I ducked, grabbing his arm the way Grampa Joji grabbed mine. I twisted hard and sent him to his knees.

Keet yelped, his face contorted. "Stop, stop!"

I let go.

Keet grabbed his wrist and staggered up. Blood drooled from his fattening lip. "You're going to die!" He turned to his gang. "Kill him!"

No one moved. Not even Dwight.

He turned back to me, his face mangled with hate. "If you think this is over then you better think again, because when I tell my—" He squeezed his eyes shut and touched his lip. "You and your family are *history*!"

"Go tell your mommy and daddy," Mose shouted.

Keet held his wrist, glaring. "Find a nice slum to move to, Jap." He backed away, looking everywhere but at the punks who came with him.

He turned and ran for the street.

"Watch your back!" Rico yelled.

Keet's gang glanced at each other, then at us, some of them shrugging, some shaking their heads. The big guy Calvin knew headed over to the canal to look down on the *Taiyo Maru*. Slowly, the others followed, tossing down their sticks and bats.

Rico came up and tapped my back. "Yeah, brah! You shamed him."

It didn't feel good. But it felt right.

I turned. "Billy—"

"It's bent but not broken." He held up the katana. There was a slight bow to it. "We can find someone who can straighten it out. You stopped him just in time. It could have been way worse."

I took the katana. It was painful to see even the smallest damage. "Thanks."

"Dad or Charlie will know where to take it."

The big guy peered into the water. "Which boat?"

"That one," Calvin said. "It's just a fishing boat."

"So what Wilson told us was a lie?"

"Does that boat look dangerous to you?" Calvin said.

"If it is, it's not going anywhere soon."

"It's not an enemy fuel boat."

"Maybe not." He glanced back toward the street. No trace of Keet Wilson. "Man, I'd hate to be in his shoes," he said. "He won't be able to look anyone in the eye." He turned to me. "And he ain't gonna be telling his dad anything."

I nodded, still so angry it spooked me. It was hard to breathe.

I mashed my lips tight. I'd get the katana fixed.

"I got work to do," I said, pushing past the big guy Calvin had faced down. I stopped and looked back at him. "You . . . you want to help?"

He raised his eyebrows, glanced at his friends.

"Tomi," Billy said, nodding toward the trees.

A jeep was heading our way.

An army jeep, with two MPs in it.

I hid the katana behind my back.

59
THE
MPs

We parted to let the jeep drive up. "What's going on here?" the driver said. "You got a problem we can help with?"

"No sir," I said. "No problem."

The MP glanced at the pontoons. "Is that military property?"

Silence.

The MPs got out of the jeep. They wore khaki U.S. Army uniforms, new bucketlike steel helmets, and black armbands with MP in white.

"We borrowed them from the marines," Billy said. "My dad got them for us. We're returning them as soon as we're . . ."

The MPs waited for more, but Billy looked down, probably wanting those words back as much as I did. Someone came up behind me and took the katana. "I hold it for you," Mose whispered.

"They're for my father's boat," I said, keeping myself from looking back at Mose. "We're . . . we're using the pontoons to bring it up off the bottom so we can take it to dry dock."

The MPs walked over and looked down on the ten boats. "All of them, or just one?" the MP asked.

"Just that one," I said, lifting my chin toward the *Taiyo Maru,* rust-colored under the wobbly water.

One MP squatted down, took off his helmet, and held it in his hands. "That's a big job, son. I see why you got all these boys here."

"Yessir."

"Mind if we watch? Not much going on for us today."

My jaw dropped. Billy and I glanced at each other.

"Sure, watch," Rico said, breaking through the crowd. "In fact, if you want, you can jump in and help us out."

The MPs grinned. One said, "Now, why would we want to spoil your fun? How'd these boats get sunk, anyway?"

It was good while it lasted, I thought. Now we've had it.

"Storm," someone said.

Ojii-chan.

I looked back at Grampa Joji straddling his bike with his feet planted in the dirt. Where had he been?

"Who are you?" the MP said, standing, putting his helmet back on.

"My son's boat," Grampa said, trying to get his English right, which gave me great relief. We didn't need those MPs to think about Japan just then.

The MP nodded. "It went down in a storm?"

"Unnh."

"What about the others?"

"Same-same."

"What?"

"They all went down the same way," I said. True.

"That right, old man?"

"Unnh."

The MP took his helmet off again and set it on the ground, then sat on it as if it were a footstool. "Take a load off, Mike," he said to the other MP. "This might be the best show we'll see all week."

Grampa laid his bike in the dirt. Mose eased over and handed him the katana. If Grampa Joji was shocked to see it, he didn't show it.

Just as we were starting to drag the pontoons to the canal, someone else showed up—Fumi.

With about twenty-five of her customers. And in the back, even Suzy.

A sailor walking next to Fumi had a half-finished tattoo on his arm. REMEMBER PEAR. Must have jumped out of the chair to come.

"Your grandpa came for us," Fumi said, striding up. "He said had trouble here."

"No trouble," I said. So he went for reinforcements!

"Good," she said, then nodded to her niece that it was okay to come closer.

"So," Fumi said. "I heard this was the big day. These boys came because I told them what you was doing and that you had trouble. But now we just going watch, ah?"

Suzy came up and stood behind her. She waved and I nodded back.

This was turning into a circus. But so what? It was a big day, the biggest day in a long time. Why not have all these strangers here? Share it. *You see, Papa? You see what we're doing? You feel it, wherever you are? Your boat is coming up!*

Rico tapped my shoulder. "Some day, ah?"

"That it is, my friend. Let's get to work."

I heard an engine cough and spit, then die.

Calvin was yanking on the compressor's pull rope, trying to start it up.

And now Ojii-chan was missing again.

"Fumi, where's Grampa?"

"He getting the boy."

"What boy?"

"Surprise."

60
GOOD
TO
GO

The big haole guy Calvin knew hovered over the compressor with his hands on his knees. "Need some muscle there, Hawaiian?"

Calvin grinned. "Hard to believe you didn't even know what you was down here to beef about."

"Yeah, well . . . sorry about that." He stuck out his hand.

Calvin grinned and slapped it. Then he rewound the pull rope.

"Wilson said it was subversive, so we came," the guy said.

Calvin looked up. "Subversive? What that means?"

"Like you're doing something for the enemy and not us."

Calvin scowled. "Well, he was wrong, ah?" He nodded toward me. "That kid who just shame your friend wants to fix up this boat for when his pops comes home."

"From where?"

Calvin glanced at me.

"He was arrested after Pearl Harbor," I said. "The navy thought he was working for Japan, helping them. But he wasn't. He was only fishing."

"And you couldn't get that cleared up?" one of the MPs said.

I shrugged. "Too much going on, those days."

"Yeah, I was at Schofield that day. That was a scary time."

I nodded. "Most of the fishermen got rounded up. But they were just peaceful working guys."

"Huh," the big haole said. "Wilson made a different story out of it."

"He's got a private war with me," I said.

"Why?"

"Ask him."

"Nah. So, how you going to float that boat, that's what I want to know?"

Calvin wagged his eyebrows. "Watch."

All along the edge of the canal a line of soldiers and sailors and the two MPs and even Keet's guys stood talking while me, Billy, Mose, Rico, Ben, and Calvin went to work. Fumi was the queen, surrounded by Suzy and her customers, laughing and joking like they were at a Hotel Street party. All we needed was the food and drinks and maybe some music.

Two sailors who knew about compressors asked if they could man it while we were in the water. "All these guys will help," one said. "Just ask."

With all these people we could probably all just get in the water and lift the boat up! "Thanks," I said. "Thank you."

"Sure thing." He squatted down by the compressor, checked the gas tank, then started it up. It sprang to life, making a terrible racket. You probably could've heard it all the way up in the mountains. The sailor nodded to the other guy to run the air hose out to us.

"Good to go!" he shouted.

Mose and Rico jumped in and took up their positions on the port side of the *Taiyo Maru*. Ben and Calvin followed, swimming over to the starboard side.

Billy and I took the air hose and swam it out.

"Do a little on one side, a little on the other," Billy said. "Back and forth so we don't tip the boat over."

"Yeah, if it flips, it's as good as gone. For us, anyway."

"I'll guide you," he said.

"Teamwork."

"Like always, huh? The Rats."

I grinned. "The Rats."

Billy and I swam the hose over to Mose and Rico's side.

"Cross your fingers." We took a deep breath, dove under, and fixed the air hose to the inflation manifold.

I came up and waved to the guys at the compressor. "Let 'er rip!"

The air hose leaped.

Air raced into the pontoon tube, the rubbery canvas writhing open. Yes! Yes!

Mose dove under to hold the air hose in place while Billy came up for air. "It's working!" he called to shore.

A cheer erupted. Fumi beamed down on us as if we were her own kids.

When the port pontoon was a quarter full, Billy ran a finger across his throat. I unhitched the air hose and swam it over to the starboard side.

Back and forth, back and forth.

The pontoons fattening.

Filling.

More.

More.

Slowly, the hull began to rise.

Even from shore they saw it shift, saw the pilot house come up out of the rusty water, saw the *Taiyo Maru* rising from its watery grave, and that was the best part, because now those sailors and army soldiers and the two MPs, and even Keet's warriors, were all cheering and clapping for every inch. Across the way, even, on the Waikiki side of the canal, another crowd was growing, coming out of the houses to see what was going on.

Slowly, the *Taiyo Maru* rose back into this world.

Not all the way, because it was full of water.

But it was enough.

Enough!

61
TO THE SEA

The pontoon tubes lifted the wheelhouse clear out of the water.

An inch still washed over the decking, but the gunnels breathed clean fresh air for the first time since the *Taiyo Maru* had gone down.

And the hull floated free.

Me, Billy, Mose, Rico, Ben, and Calvin climbed aboard and stood ankle-deep on deck with our fists in the air, the crowd clapping and hooting down on us.

We did it!

While all that celebrating was going on, I glanced down the canal toward the ocean. A boat was working its way up-river.

I squinted.

What?

Closer, closer.

No. Can't be. But how—

Standing on the bow of a boat half the size of the *Taiyo Maru* was Grampa Joji. Behind him were two Kaka'ako boys—Ichiro Frankie Fujita and Herbie Okubo.

So *Herbie* was the boy Grampa went to get. You crabby, grumpy, cranky, brilliant old goat. A lump grew in my throat as I watched them ease toward us, the engine tok-tok-tokking on water as smooth as silk.

Herbie waved, walking his boat up. "Need a tow?"

I was too choked up to answer, so I nodded and tapped Billy to answer for me. "Thought you'd never ask," he said.

Herbie edged the boat in closer and put it in neutral, let it glide the rest of the way. Bow bumped bow.

Ichiro, or I should say Frankie, handed a coiled rope forward to Grampa on the bow. Grampa tossed it to me. I caught it and pulled Herbie's boat alongside the *Taiyo Maru*.

"Ojii-chan," I said, then couldn't go on.

"Unnnh."

I motioned for him to step over onto Papa's sampan. "Come, Ojii-chan," I managed to say. "Ride with us."

Herbie handed Grampa the katana, which was on deck near his feet.

Grampa nodded, a slight bow, rare for an old man to give a boy.

Ben and Calvin jumped off and swam to shore.

"Boy," Fumi called. "Wait for me . . . I be right back." She grabbed one of the sailors and scurried back toward the trees and the street.

Grampa Joji stepped over onto the *Taiyo Maru* and

slogged through the water to the wheelhouse. The look on his face was as always, blank and stern. As he passed by he tapped my shoulder, not even glancing at me.

I breathed deep and turned away.

Fumi came hurrying back, with the sailor carrying two rickety wooden chairs. She must know everyone on this island, I thought.

"Suzy," she called. "Go home the solja boys. They take good care of you."

Suzy waved her off. "Don't worry, Aunty. I'll be fine."

Fumi glanced at the sailor, hooking her thumb at Suzy. "You watch out her, ah?"

The sailor nodded.

Fumi turned to Ben and Calvin. "You . . . big boys. Take me and this chairs to the boat."

Calvin grinned and took the chairs, handed them to Ben, who waded out, then swam them to the *Taiyo Maru*. Mose took them aboard and set them up on the deck.

Calvin went back to shore.

"Okay, old lady. Your turn."

"Who you calling old lady?"

Calvin tipped his head to the side, quick-thinking. "I said that? I never said that." Fumi rapped his head with her knuckles, making Calvin grin.

She sat between Ben and Calvin, who stood shoulder to shoulder. They swam her out and lifted her aboard, soaked to her waist.

"No worry about the compressor and the pontoons," Calvin said to me. "We take um home. Talk later, ah?"

"Yeah," I squeaked. I reached down to shake his hand.

Calvin reached up and shook, then slapped the gunnel. "Take her home, skippa."

Me, Billy, Mose, and Rico climbed over onto Herbie's small sampan.

"Rico," I said. "Go up the bow, lead the way. You paid the most for this."

Rico saluted and crabbed his way forward to stand on the bow, like Sanji used to. He turned back and grinned.

"Look at that fool," Mose said.

"If he's a fool, then I want to be one too," I said.

"Yeah."

Herbie powered forward, easing the boat away, heading toward the ocean and Kewalo Basin.

I turned and stood with my hands on my hips, looking back at Fumi and Grampa Joji sitting side by side in those rickety chairs, facing into the breeze. The katana lay across Ojii-chan's knees, his face expressionless. If I didn't know him I'd have thought he was angry. But that cranky look was just his way of looking peaceful. He was content. Even with the bent katana.

I frowned. How many more battles stood between me and the day Papa would finally come home? And what about Grampa Joji? Would he stay strong? And then there was Keet Wilson. Who could get us kicked out of our home.

I closed my eyes. So much trouble I had caused for my family. Was all this worth it? *Papa?*

When I opened my eyes Ojii-chan was staring at me, as if he'd been reading my mind. His scowl and unwavering eyes said, *No matter what comes, boy, we going be all right.*

I waved.

Fumi waved back, smiling. Ojii-chan managed to lift his chin.

Herbie laughed. "Your grampa, he's tough."

"The toughest guy I know," I said.

Herbie nodded. "No worry, ah? We can bring that boat back to life."

"We just did, Herbie . . . we just did."

Grampa shooed us on with his wrinkled skeleton hand, waving us out toward the sea.

"We going, old man," I called. "Confonnit!"

GLOSSARY

BMTC—Businessmen's Military Training Corps
MP—military police
VVV—Varsity Victory Volunteers

HAWAIIAN
hanabatas—boogers (Hawaiian pidgin)
haole—foreigner; Caucasian; white person
Imua!—Onward! Charge!
mu'umu'u—loose-fitting Hawaiian dress
okole—rear end
Shaka sign—hand sign meaning "take it easy," "thanks,"
"how's it?"

JAPANESE
Anohito wa okane motterukara.—She's getting rich.
butsudan—Buddhist altar
Fumi wa kimae ga iihito nandakara.—
Fumi is a nice lady.
furoshiki—cloth wrapper
Gaman.—Endure, persevere.
hato poppo—pigeons
Hinamatsuri—Girls' Festival (also called Dolls' Festival)
Irasshaimase.—Please come in.
katana—samurai sword
Kessite akirameruna.—Don't ever give up.
"Kimigayo"—national anthem of Japan

koi-nobori—a carp streamer

Meueno hitoni mukatte nanda sonotaidowa!—
Show some respect when you talk to an older person!

Mon dai nai.—No problem.

musubi—rice ball

Ojima shimashita.—Sorry to have intruded.

onna hitorito kikai ichidai ka—one girl, one machine

Shooshoo omachi kudasai.—Please wait a moment.

Tango-no-Sekku—Boys' Festival

tatami mat—a mat made from grasses

udon—noodle soup

GRAHAM SALISBURY's family has lived in the Hawaiian Islands since the early 1800s. He grew up on Oahu and Hawaii and graduated from California State University. He received an MFA from Vermont College of Norwich University, where he was a member of the founding faculty of the MFA program in writing for children. He lives with his family in Portland, Oregon.

Graham Salisbury's books have garnered many prizes. *Blue Skin of the Sea* won the Bank Street Child Study Association Award and the Oregon Book Award; *Under the Blood-Red Sun* won the Scott O'Dell Award for Historical Fiction, the Oregon Book Award, Hawaii's Nene Award, and the California Young Reader Medal; *Shark Bait* won the Oregon Book Award and a *Parents' Choice* Silver Honor; *Lord of the Deep* won the *Boston Globe–Horn Book* Award for fiction. *Jungle Dogs* was an ALA Best Book for Young Adults, and *Island Boyz: Stories* was a *Booklist* Editors' Choice. His most recent book was *Eyes of the Emperor,* an ALA Best Book for Young Adults and an ALA Notable Book.

Graham Salisbury has been a recipient of the John Unterecker Award for Fiction and the PEN/Norma Klein Award.

GRAHAM SALISBURY

HOUSE OF THE
RED FISH

A READERS GUIDE

"Salisbury's intimate understanding of Hawaii's
unique cultural landscape permeates his work.
He weaves history, camaraderie, and a coming of age
story that connects brilliantly with today's kids."
—*The Honolulu Advertiser*

"A book that will be passed eagerly from
reader to reader for years to come."
—*The Plain Deuler* (Cleveland)

1. Graham Salisbury starts *House of the Red Fish* with a scene from Tomi's life before his father was arrested. Why do you think the author does this? What is the difference between the life that Tomi leads now and his life before the arrest?

2. Tomi has a deep sentimental attachment to his father's boat, the *Taiyo Maru*. Raising it is a tough job, but once he sets his mind on it, he can think of little else. Do you think he's right to risk so much to save the boat?

3. Tomi knows that if Papa had been home, he would have told Tomi not to fight Keet Wilson or anyone who is hostile to the Japanese and Japanese American citizens of Hawaii. Papa would have said, *"Don't shame the family. Be helpful, be generous, be accepting"* (page 15). But Tomi sees Grampa Joji, who's over seventy, as a fighter. What do you think of Papa's and Grampa Joji's different attitudes toward fighting? Do you think Tomi fights back against Keet Wilson in an honorable way?

4. Tomi buries his *katana,* or samurai sword, so that it won't be taken away. Later he discovers that Keet Wilson has stolen it. If your family was threatened, what possession would you try to save? Is Tomi right to sneak into Keet's room and try to get the katana back? Do you think Tomi's mother is right in not allowing him to take the katana?

5. Mr. Ramos helps Tomi find out the laws that pertain to raising the boat. Why do you think Mr. Ramos helps Tomi? Was Rico right to tell Mr. Ramos about their project?

6. Mr. Wilson seems to trust Tomi's mother, but on pages 171 and 172 he says that Tomi's grandfather should have been left in jail and that Tomi's family is "an annoyance and, frankly, a worry to everyone around here." Can you understand Mr. Wilson's prejudice? Do you think he's justified in worrying?

7. Keet Wilson tries to sabotage Tomi's mission to bring up the boat. Why does he do this? Why does he care so much about what Tomi does and disagree with Tomi's plan for Papa's boat? Why do you think Keet chooses Tomi to bully?

8. What do you think of the end of the book? Will Tomi's father be proud of him?

To read Graham Salisbury's answers
to these questions, visit his Web site:
www.grahamsalisbury.com

IN HIS
OWN WORDS

A CONVERSATION WITH
GRAHAM SALISBURY

JEFF PFEFFER

Q: What inspired you to write this story? Why does Tomi appeal to you as a protagonist?

A: Tomi appeals to me most in the context of his family and friends. I love the whole lot of them, how they blend, how they fit together. Tomi himself, however, appeals to me because he's a fighter. I like that. Maybe I see something in him that I would hope to see in myself, were I in his shoes. I just like his dogged determination and refusal to give in or give up. Elmore Leonard wrote a book called *Valdez Is Coming.* It's one of my all-time favorite books. Valdez is a man who is relentless in the pursuit of justice. Nothing can stop him, even the risk of death. It is this same pursuit of justice that drives Tomi. Never, never, never give up. I like that.

Q: In two of your other books, *Under the Blood-Red Sun* and *Eyes of the Emperor,* you've also written about Japanese Americans living in Hawaii and the prejudice they face during World War II. Why do this era and setting hold such appeal for you as a writer?

A: The story of the American of Japanese ancestry, in Hawaii and on the mainland, is a powerful one. The story of how one group, especially one so loyal to the American way of life, could be so wrongfully treated tells of some basic fear that lives in the American psyche. We are a good people. We are generous and forgiving. Yet we own some kind of deep-rooted fear that has, at times, ripped the goodness and generosity right out of our hearts. Having grown up in the islands, I know somewhat of the Japanese living there. I know that as a whole they are as good and generous and accepting as

5

any other decent American. When I look at what our government did to them in World War II, and how they, the JAs, fought to prove their loyalty to that very same government, I am impressed. Actually, I am impressed and fascinated. Would I have had such courage? Would you?

Q: What was the most difficult part of writing this book?
A: The first draft. First drafts are always the toughest part of any book for me. That's because I am making something out of nothing. But the one item of writing craft that I know with certainty is this: I can fix it. I love revision, thank heaven. Revision is where I can sit back and live the story a bit, sort of climb into it and explore it on deeper levels. But that first draft is a bear, a grizzly. No, Bigfoot.

Q: What will happen to Tomi and his friends and family next?
A: I sort of have to wait and see what will happen to them. I have a general idea of what I would like to see happen, but stories have a way of telling themselves once I get into them, no matter how tightly I plot and plan. The characters and events sometimes surprise me, which I love. Surprise is the element of writing that most fascinates me . . . and keeps me at this rather difficult (and oh so rewarding) occupation.

Q: What do you like best about being a writer?
A: Just as I stated above: I love the magic that happens when I am working (the surprises that come out of nowhere). Hand in hand with writing surprises is the

absolute thrill of discovering a new story that would be stunning to tell. *Eyes of the Emperor* was one of those thrills, those stories. When I first discovered it (in a three-page essay written by one of the Cat Island men, Raymond Nosaka), it grabbed me and shook me and said You *have to tell this story!* Now, that's exciting stuff.

Q: Tell us about your writing habits.
A: I am a morning person. I do my best work before 10 a.m. I get up at 4:45 every weekday. I work best when I am away from my e-mail (which is so much easier than *working!*). So before I go to my studio (a 900-square-foot cabana built on a pier out over a lake), I go to any one of several favorite coffee shops and work there. Sometimes I write first drafts in longhand and revise on my Mac. Sometimes I do it all on my laptop. I work in coffee shops because I like the white noise of other people bustling about. I try my best to write every day except weekends, which I reserve for my family. Discipline is a key element. I am not a genius. I am a trudger. I make it happen. There is no other way.

Q: Do you eat snacks while you write?
A: No. I get too deep down into my imagination to think about snacks (but I do drink one cup of coffee a day— a twelve-ounce Americano with a tad of nonfat milk stirred in). When I surface, I'm usually famished and ready to hit the gym. I eat lunch after the gym, and sometimes in the hot months get a Jamba Juice (Orange Dream Machine) or iced green tea as I head back to work.

Q: Do you listen to music while writing?
A: Never—if I'm writing at my cabana. I may listen to very soft, very calm instrumental music while revising, but never when involved in a first draft. The one exception to this took place when I was writing the first draft of a short story called "Angel-Baby," when I listened to Houston Person's luxurious rendering of "But Beautiful" (on his CD called *My Romance*). You will see why if you read that story (it's in my short story collection *Island Boyz*). However, when I write in coffee shops, there is always music. White noise to me. After I have finished a book and am celebrating, I crank the radio in my car and listen to something that rocks!

Q: How much research do you have to do before writing a book? Where do you do it?
A: It all depends on the project. For the war books, research is key. I want my facts to be as accurate as possible. I do my best research in the same place I do my best writing—in coffee shops, except when I need to ply the Net (I don't do coffee shop hot spots, because I want to keep the Net out of that workspace). If I need to search the Internet, I go to my cabana and work there. I also have access to a research professional when the research demands an expertise I don't have. She lives in Idaho and is wonderful. But the best kind of research I can do (if possible) is primary research, where I interview people who were actually present during whatever piece of history I am writing about. *That* is a thrill!

Q: Do you ever get writer's block?
A: I get lazy, I get stuck, I dink around—but I never get writer's block. Writer's block to me is one thing and one thing only: procrastination. I try to keep moving ahead, even if I hate what I'm producing. You see, I have learned something valuable over my years of writing: whatever drivel I produce, I can make it better. I work hard. Most of the time.

Q: As a writer, what is your greatest fear? Your greatest obstacle?
A: As a writer I have few fears. However, I do have a good deal of self-doubt. Am I really good enough to continue writing stories of value for young readers? So far, I believe I am (any writer has to have that self-belief to succeed). I guess if I have a fear at all, it would be the fear of losing that confidence. Yeah, that would be it.

Q: How much rewriting and revising do you do?
A: A lot! Over and over and over until I think it sings. Then I send it to my editor and she sends it back saying, "You can do better." And she's always right. I can, and do. God bless good editors, and I have one of the best ever. Revise, revise, revise. It will shower you with sparkling diamonds every time.

Eyes of the Emperor
Graham Salisbury
978-0-440-22956-8

Eddy Okubo lies about his age and joins the army in his hometown, Honolulu, only weeks before the Japanese bomb Pearl Harbor. Suddenly, Americans see him as the enemy. Even the U.S. Army doubts the loyalty of Japanese American enlisted men.
Then Eddy and a small band of Japanese American soldiers are sent on a secret mission to a small island. They are given a special job, one that only they can do.

The Watsons Go to Birmingham—1963
Christopher Paul Curtis
978-0-440-41412-4

Nine-year-old Kenny lives with his middle-class black family, the Weird Watsons of Flint, Michigan. When Kenny's thirteen-year-old brother, Byron, gets to be too much trouble, they head south to Birmingham to visit Grandma, the one person who can shape him up. And they happen to be in Birmingham when Grandma's church is bombed.

Before We Were Free
Julia Alvarez
978-0-440-23784-6

Under a dictatorship in the Dominican Republic in 1960, young Anita lives through a fight for freedom that changes her world forever.

Cuba 15
Nancy Osa
978-0-385-73233-8

Violet Paz's upcoming *quinceañero,* a girl's traditional fifteenth-birthday coming-of-age ceremony, awakens her interest in her Cuban roots—and sparks a fire of conflicting feelings about Cuba within her family.

Counting Stars • David Almond • 978-0-440-41826-9
With stories that shimmer and vibrate in the bright heat of memory, David Almond creates a glowing mosaic of his life growing up in a large, loving Catholic family in north-eastern England.

Heaven Eyes • David Almond • 978-0-440-22910-0
Erin Law and her friends in the orphanage are labeled Damaged Children. They run away one night, traveling down-river on a raft. What they find on their journey is stranger than you can imagine.

The Sisterhood of the Traveling Pants • Ann Brashares
978-0-385-73058-7
Over a few bags of cheese puffs, four girls decide to form a sisterhood and take the vow of the Sisterhood of the Traveling Pants. The next morning, they say goodbye. And then the journey of the Pants, and the most memorable summer of their lives, begin.

A Great and Terrible Beauty • Libba Bray
978-0-385-73231-4
Sixteen-year-old Gemma Doyle is sent to the Spence Academy in London after tragedy strikes her family in India. Lonely, guilt-ridden, and prone to visions of the future that have an uncomfortable habit of coming true, Gemma finds her reception a chilly one. But at Spence, Gemma's power to attract the supernatural unfolds; she becomes entangled with the school's most powerful girls and discovers her mother's connection to a shadowy group called the Order. A curl-up-under-the-covers Victorian gothic.

READERS CIRCLE BOOKS

Walking Naked • Alyssa Brugman • 978-0-440-23832-4
Megan doesn't know a thing about Perdita, since she would never dream of talking to her. Only when the two girls are thrown together in detention does Megan begin to see Perdita as more than the school outcast. Slowly, Megan finds herself drawn into a challenging almost-friendship.

Colibrí • Ann Cameron • 978-0-440-42052-1
At age four, Colibrí was kidnapped from her parents in Guatemala City, and ever since then she's traveled with Uncle, who believes Colibrí will lead him to treasure. Danger mounts as Uncle grows desperate for his fortune—and as Colibrí grows daring in seeking her freedom.

The Chocolate War • Robert Cormier • 978-0-375-82987-1
Jerry Renault dares to disturb the universe in this ground-breaking and now classic novel, an unflinching portrait of corruption and cruelty in a boys' prep school.

Bud, Not Buddy • Christopher Paul Curtis
978-0-553-49410-5
Ten-year-old Bud's momma never told him who his father was, but she left a clue: flyers advertising Herman E. Calloway and his famous band. Bud's got an idea that those flyers will lead him to his father. Once he decides to hit the road and find this mystery man, nothing can stop him.

Dr. Franklin's Island • Ann Halam • 978-0-440-23781-5
A plane crash leaves Semi, Miranda, and Arnie stranded on a tropical island, totally alone. Or so they think. Dr. Franklin is a mad scientist who has set up his laboratory on the island, and the three teens are perfect subjects for his frightening experiments in genetic engineering.

Keeper of the Night • Kimberly Willis Holt
978-0-553-49441-9
Living on the island of Guam, a place lush with memories and tradition, young Isabel struggles to protect her family and cope with growing up after her mother's suicide.

When Zachary Beaver Came to Town • Kimberly Willis Holt
978-0-440-23841-6
Toby's small, sleepy Texas town is about to get a jolt with the arrival of Zachary Beaver, billed as the fattest boy in the world. Toby is in for a summer unlike any other—a summer sure to change his life.

The Parallel Universe of Liars • Kathleen Jeffrie Johnson
978-0-440-23852-2
Surrounded by superficiality, infidelity, and lies, Robin, a self-described chunk, isn't sure what to make of her hunky neighbor's sexual advances, or of the attention paid her by a new boy in town who seems to notice more than her body.

Ghost Boy • Iain Lawrence • 978-0-440-41668-5
Fourteen-year-old Harold Kline is an albino—an outcast. When the circus comes to town, Harold runs off to join it in hopes of discovering who he is and what he wants in life. Is he a circus freak or just a normal guy?

The Lightkeeper's Daughter • Iain Lawrence
978-0-385-73127-0
Imagine growing up on a tiny island with no one but your family. For Squid McCrae, returning to the island after three years away unleashes a storm of bittersweet memories, revelations, and accusations surrounding her brother's death.

Girl, 15, Charming but Insane • Sue Limb
978-0-385-73215-4
With her hilariously active imagination, Jess Jordan has a tendency to complicate her life, but now, as she's finally getting closer to her crush, she's determined to keep things under control. Readers will fall in love with Sue Limb's insanely optimistic heroine.

The Silent Boy • Lois Lowry • 978-0-440-41980-8
When tragedy strikes a small turn-of-the-century town, only Katy realizes what the gentle, silent boy did for his family. He meant to help, not harm. It didn't turn out that way.

Shades of Simon Gray • Joyce McDonald
978-0-440-22804-2
Simon is the ideal teenager—smart, reliable, hardworking, trustworthy. Or is he? After Simon's car crashes into a tree and he slips into a coma, another portrait of him begins to emerge.

Zipped • Laura and Tom McNeal • 978-0-375-83098-3
In a suspenseful novel of betrayal, forgiveness, and first love, fifteen-year-old Mick Nichols opens an e-mail he was never meant to see—and learns a terrible secret.

Harmony • Rita Murphy • 978-0-440-22923-0
Power is coursing through Harmony—the power to affect the universe with her energy. This is a frightening gift for a girl who has always hated being different, and Harmony must decide whether to hide her abilities or embrace the consequences—good and bad—of her full strength.

Her Father's Daughter • Mollie Poupeney
978-0-440-22879-0
As she matures from a feisty tomboy of seven to a spirited young woman of fourteen, Maggie discovers that the only constant in her life of endless new homes and new faces is her ever-emerging sense of herself.

Pool Boy • Michael Simmons • 978-0-385-73196-6
Brett Gerson is the kind of guy you love to hate—until his father is thrown in prison and Brett has to give up the good life. That's when some swimming pools enter his world and change everything.

Milkweed • Jerry Spinelli • 978-0-440-42005-7
He's a boy called Jew. Gypsy. Stopthief. Runt. He's a boy who lives in the streets of Warsaw. He's a boy who wants to be a Nazi someday, with tall, shiny jackboots of his own. Until the day that suddenly makes him change his mind—the day he realizes it's safest of all to be nobody.

Stargirl • Jerry Spinelli • 978-0-440-41677-7
Stargirl. From the day she arrives at quiet Mica High in a burst of color and sound, the hallways hum with the murmur of "Stargirl, Stargirl." The students are enchanted. Then they turn on her.

Shabanu: Daughter of the Wind • Suzanne Fisher Staples
978-0-440-23856-0
Life is both sweet and cruel to strong-willed young Shabanu, whose home is the windswept Cholistan Desert of Pakistan. She must reconcile her duty to her family and the stirrings of her own heart in this Newbery Honor–winning modern-day classic.

The Gospel According to Larry • Janet Tashjian
978-0-440-23792-1
Josh Swensen's virtual alter ego, Larry, becomes a huge media sensation. While it seems as if the whole world is trying to figure out Larry's true identity, Josh feels trapped inside his own creation.

Memories of Summer • Ruth White • 978-0-440-22921-6
In 1955, thirteen-year-old Lyric describes her older sister Summer's descent into mental illness, telling Summer's story with humor, courage, and love.